# MEAT PHOTO

## C.V. HUNT & ANDERSEN PRUNTY

*For Neal*
*A guy who knows how to take a joke.*

# 1

**K**YLE BAKER SHUT THE DOOR on his sick wife and entered the living room. The boy, Chad, was on the couch, as always. He sat in his sweatpants and dirty t-shirt, his eyes only half open.

"I'm going out," Kyle said. "I should be back by morning."

"You're going to see *him*, aren't you?"

Kyle was surprised the boy said anything.

"It's really none of your business, but yes. I'm going to hang out with Tony. He's a lot more fun than you."

"He's *younger* than me."

"He's eleven, but he's mature for his age. You're in the same class so I'm sure you know this."

"What about—?"

"Your mother'll be fine. She's going to start screaming about how hungry she is, but don't fall for it. I left a bag of Munch in there with her. If she needs something to eat, she can eat that. Nobody's too good for Munch. Besides, regardless of what she says, she loves Munch." Kyle chuckled, a wistful look in his eye. "Everybody loves Munch."

Kyle expected Chad to come back with something, even though

his critical-thinking skills were not the best. Chad did open his mouth but nothing came out.

"I don't know why you act so surprised every time I want to leave," Kyle said. "It's not like there's anything keeping me here. I've told you I realized I made a mistake by having you, or rather by keeping you. We should have put you up for adoption and tried again. I knew you weren't going to fit our vibe and now look at us. Barely a family. I mean, look, you're too lazy to even turn on the TV or play video games like most kids your age."

It was true. Chad sat on the couch with his hands on his lap, his eyes barely open, his face pointed at a blank TV screen.

"I'm too tired to keep my eyes open," Chad said. "You know that."

"Then maybe you need to get more rest."

"There's too much stuff on my bed."

Kyle tugged on the nostril hairs he let grow out of one nostril only. He thought every middle-aged man needed a quirk and this one seemed simple and affordable. He knew a lot of people thought it was gross or weird, but Tony thought it was great.

"See," Kyle said, "that's where Tony is different than you. His bed is always covered in stuff but he doesn't seem tired at all. Ever. He has the same energy I had when I was eleven. Real vintage energy."

"Whatever."

"Yeah, exactly . . . whatever."

And with that, Kyle walked out the front door.

# 2

**A**S SOON AS CHAD HEARD his dad fire up the ancient LeBaron and back out of the driveway, he felt free. He could do anything. He continued to sit on the couch, his eyes fully closing periodically. He thought about lying down on the couch but it seemed like too much work. He didn't know how long he sat there. There was a clock above the TV, but he didn't want to lift his head far enough to look at it so he decided he would just sit there until his dad came back in the morning. Then he would know it was time to go to school. Mrs. Davis was nice. She let him sleep at his desk. His desk at school was also covered in things but it was easier to just rake it onto the floor. It's what all the kids did. Nobody gave a shit.

Sometimes Chad tried to make himself stop breathing but he couldn't get himself to fully lose consciousness and gave up after a while.

Just when he felt like he was getting into the rhythm of things, his mother shouted from the bedroom.

"Chad! Chad! *Chaaaad!*"

He took a deep, shaky breath, pretty sure he was going to have a panic attack if he stood up. But what was the alternative? To sit and listen to his mother yell? Maybe if he yelled back, she'd stop screaming.

It took a lot of work, but Chad managed to summon the lung capacity to shout, "Dad said you have some Munch! I don't know how to cook!" His voice broke on the last word, which had been happening a lot lately as puberty settled in.

"Come here NOW!" she shouted.

Trying to support himself on the edge of the couch, Chad managed to stand up. The room swam around him and he was pretty sure he was going to fall down. If he fell down, he'd have to just lie there. Getting up from the couch was hard enough. Getting up all the way from the floor would be nearly impossible. He slowly crossed the small living room and went down the narrow hall to his mother's room. He turned the knob, half-expecting it to be locked. His father was the only one with the key. Even attempting to open the door if it was locked seemed like a waste of energy so he hoped it wasn't, for his and his mother's sake.

He turned the knob and the door swung inward.

His mother lay in the bed, Munch crumbs all down the front of her nightgown. She lay on her back, rigid, clutching something in her hands. She couldn't sit up anymore.

"What do you want?" Chad said.

"What is it?" she said.

"Huh?"

She thrust the thing in her hands at him. He took a step toward her, not wanting to take more steps than necessary. He held out his hand to reach for the piece of paper or photo or whatever but, unfortunately, had to take another step. He was sure all this physical exertion was shaving minutes off his life.

He took it and turned it around so he could see what was on the front.

"What is it?" His mother sounded scared. Or angry. He wasn't really sure which. He'd never been good at reading emotions.

The photo was blurry at first but if he opened his eyes a little further, he could make it out better.

"Looks like," he said, "a picture of meat."

"Why? Why is it in this house?"

Chad could sense her getting worked up. He didn't want to have to call 911 again.

"Probably . . . Dad? Maybe?" There were a lot of other things he could say but his jaws got tired if he talked too much. Sometimes his tongue felt too big.

4

"Maybe he can explain it then. Where is that horrible man?"

"He's at . . . Tony's?"

"That's all he can talk about. Tony. Fuck Tony."

Chad didn't laugh because he had forgotten how. He tried to a couple of times but it didn't work. It made his face hurt.

"Stop making that weird face," his mother said.

Chad closed his mouth and decided he would never try laughing again. "You want me to throw it away?"

His mother didn't say anything for a while and Chad wondered if he'd said his words right. While it was exhausting, he decided to try again. Sometimes he thought he was talking but nothing came out.

"You want me to throw it away?"

"I want you to stick it up your father's ass."

Chad had to think about this. How it would happen. If it was even possible. If this was something a son should do to his father. He thought about his father's asshole, how nasty it probably was.

"I don't think he's coming back until morning," he said.

"Throw it in the trash then. Burn it. I don't care."

*Burn it.*

It had been a long time since Chad had burned anything but this sounded like the most exciting course of action. Fire always made him feel more alive even though it was often a lot of work to start. He'd have to look for matches or a lighter or something. The stove had been repossessed and he didn't know what putting it in the microwave would do. He was pretty sure Tony probably had a lighter. He was the only kid in the elementary school who still smoked. It would really be an adventure. Just like in the video games he used to play until his hands started hurting too bad. It was a quest. The photo needed burning, but first he had to procure something that could burn it. Once it was burned, there would probably be another world or another level or something that opened up. Maybe the photo would turn into a ghost or a demon or something. For the first time in a while, he started to feel a glimmer of hope.

The rustle of the Munch bag and his mother's chewing disrupted him from his thoughts.

"Get the fuck out of here," his mother said. "Let me Munch in peace."

Too tired to turn around, Chad backed out of the room holding the meat photo in both hands, staring at the intricacies of the marbled fat and glistening, deep red muscle tissue.

# 3

CHAD HAD FORGOTTEN WHAT HE was supposed to
be doing. He recalled his mother handing him the photo of
meat and telling him to do something with it, but his capacity
to remember things was as stunted as his drive to do anything other
than sit on the sofa, which was where he was now, holding the photo
and staring at it with half-opened eyes.

He was pretty sure his mother had told him to shove the photo
up his ass, or his father's, but he couldn't be sure. That didn't sound
right. Maybe she'd told him to burn the house down? That couldn't
be right either. Chad's thoughts were a jumbled mess and it hurt to
think. It hurt to move. He was so mesmerized by the meat in the
photo he couldn't concentrate on much else. And his arms were
growing tired of holding the photo.

Chad dropped his arms to his sides and let his head slump to his
chest so he could continue to stare at the photo now resting on his
lap. His shirt was too tight and had ridden up, exposing his bulging
stomach, partially built from his laziness and partially from the bags
of Munch he pilfered from his mother's stash when no one was looking. For as much as she would complain about Munch from time to
time, she sure did eat a lot of it. The band of his underwear was

exposed above the waistline of his sweatpants. The elasticated band was more than halfway detached from his underwear and an idea, something not common for Chad, came to him.

Chad set the photo on the sofa and tore his eyes from it. It was painful to look away from it, but doing anything felt painful to Chad. He grabbed the waistband of his underwear and pulled. The effort was exhausting and he wanted to stop, but something compelled him to follow through. He thought he might actually be able to sleep after his struggles and yanked on the band, giving himself a wedgie in the process, until the band came free.

He had to take a breather once he was done struggling. His arms ached from the exertion and he closed his eyes. He may have fallen asleep for a minute before he pulled the band up over his head, doubled it because it was stretched out from his girth, and placed it around his forehead like a sweatband. Chad picked up the photo and stared at it again, his arm trembling under the weight of the paper.

The meat swam before his eyes. It moved like the ocean. He couldn't be sure but he thought it was whispering. He held the photo to his ear.

"Meat photo," it said.

"Huh?"

"Meat photo."

"Meat photo." He turned the photo over. The words "meat" and "1987" and "Neal" were inscribed on the back and he knew for certain what he needed to do.

**4**

**K**YLE KNOCKED ON THE DOOR of Tony's house. He looked around at all the trash in the front yard illuminated by the sickly yellow glow emanating from the porch light and wondered what Tony's mom was doing with all of it. He pounded on the door with his fist and shouted, "Tony!"

A wet hack came from the other side of the door and someone shouted, "I'm comin', I'm comin'! Jesus fuckin' Christ! Hold you're fuckin' horses!"

Kyle couldn't be sure if the voice was male or female. It was probably Tony's mom but it could be one of her many lovers. It was hard to tell. Tony always hated his mom's boyfriends and would tell his mom they molested him so she would throw them out. Tony told him he wanted to be the man of the house. Kyle thought Tony was really clever. More wet coughs and the door opened. The door stopped abruptly after a foot and was caught by one of the mounds of trash just inside the house.

A large, hangdog woman with disheveled hair, wearing a see-through slip, appeared in the small opening of the door—Tony's mother. A half-smoked cigarette hung from her bottom lip and she hacked into her fist before shouting, "What do ya want?"

"Is Tony here?"

"Tony?!"

"Yes. Your son?"

"I know who my son is! I'm not a fuckin' moron!"

Kyle stroked his nostril hair. "I didn't say you were, ma'am. I was supposed to meet Tony. We were gonna go out and fuck some shit up."

"What do ya want with my son?!" The force of her shouting caused her to cough so hard her cigarette shot from her mouth, hit Kyle in the chest, and dropped to the ground.

Tony's mom stared at the nearly spent cigarette forlornly. Kyle looked at his shirt to see the small burn among several food stains before staring at the cigarette also. A minute passed as the two watched the cigarette burn down to the filter. Kyle finally had the notion to step on it and tamp it out.

Kyle tried to shout into the house but ended up shouting into Tony's mother's face, "Tony! Let's fuck some shit up! Your mom is being a cunt! With a capital K!"

Kyle pushed on the door to shove the trash back, causing a pile of junk stacked to the ceiling to come crashing down on Tony's mom. The clutter kept coming and avalanched out the front door of the home, knocking Kyle on his ass and partially burying him.

"Tony!" Kyle shouted. "Your mom is trying to kill me!"

A crash sounded somewhere deep within the house, followed by hurried footsteps. More sounds of things falling over came from within the house. There was some muffled cursing and shouts coming from the pile of junk that had been expelled out the front door. Kyle was pretty sure it was Tony's mom, but she was a barrier between Kyle and Tony's bromance and Kyle thought it best if he didn't help her.

Tony clambered over the stuff filling the doorway. There was a silver substance around his mouth and his eyes were glazed over. In one hand he gripped a paper bag and in his other hand he held a colorful paper. Tony tripped over a child's tricycle and landed beside Kyle. Kyle pushed the trash off his legs and sat up.

"Sorry it took me so long," Tony said. "I was jerking off to this awesome meat photo I found." He laughed, held the paper bag over his mouth and nose, and breathed deeply. He pulled the deflated bag from his face, crumpled it, and tossed it into the yard with the rest of the trash. "I guess you can say . . . I was beating my meat."

# 5

ROSA DANIELS DIDN'T KNOW ABOUT the guy using her bathroom. She'd met him at the Dollar General. He was at least twenty years older than her but beggars couldn't be choosers. It had been so long since Rosa had been on a date, she unhesitatingly said yes when Todd asked if she wanted to go to dinner with him. Now she sat on the couch, waiting for him, feeling like she'd done most of the talking and that the night hadn't been going well so far.

She had thought Todd would take her to a nice sit-down restaurant, but he had taken her through the drive-thru at Taco Bell, where he had strongly encouraged her to order off the value menu. She wondered how someone his age could be so poor but told herself he was probably an artist of some kind. They sat in the parking lot and ate their food. She talked around mouthfuls while Todd fidgeted with the radio knob, landing on a station that was nothing but static.

"This one's my favorite." A tooth fell out of his mouth when he spoke, landing in the wrapper of his bean burrito. He plucked it up and tossed it out the window without even acknowledging it had fallen out of his mouth.

He'd lost one more tooth by the time they were finished.

After tossing the wrappers and bag into the back floorboard, he spent a long time poorly rolling a cigarette with shaky hands. He offered it to her.

"Oh," she said. "No thanks. I don't smoke anymore."

He grunted and lit up, the acrid smoke filling the car. She wanted to roll down a window but he said none of them worked.

"You gonna host?" he said.

She had no idea what he meant.

"Host what?" she said.

"Me." He did his best to smile but it looked more ghoulish than anything. A few of his teeth wiggled as his lips passed over them.

"I don't . . ."

"I guess it's like saying your place or mine. I can't host 'cause my place is undergoing some renovations."

"Oh . . . you . . . wanna come back to my place?"

"I thought you'd never ask."

He slapped her hard on the thigh, causing her to jump, and she was certain there would be a bruise in the morning. The car started on the third attempt, and they were on their way back to her cramped studio in the trashy section of town.

Rosa wondered if Todd would want to have sex with her. Just the thought of it made her cheeks flush. It had been so long she knew she would say yes even though she wasn't particularly attracted to Todd. She imagined them in her bed, him on top of her, teeth raining down as he worked away. This made her even more aroused. Her first sexual encounter had been with one of her grandfather's friends who had no teeth at all. She wanted to ask Todd if he would let her extract the remainder of his teeth but felt like it was too soon. She thought about how different her life would be if she'd gotten into dentistry instead of taking a job at the Dollar General.

If he spent any more time in the bathroom, she was going to lose interest completely or pass out. Just when she thought her blood sugar couldn't spike any further, Todd came out of the bathroom.

He was completely naked.

"You're pretty forward," she said. "I like it."

He worked his small penis in his hand.

"Sorry I took so long," he said. "I used your shower. Mine ain't been workin' too well."

She noticed he'd lost a couple more teeth since disappearing into the bathroom and hoped she would find them trapped by the drain in the tub.

"Is that other dude always in your bathroom?" he said.

It took Rosa a second to process this. A dude in her bathroom? Her burgeoning lust was replaced with a cold fear.

"There's a guy in my bathroom?" She tried not to sound as shocked as she felt.

"Yeah," Todd said. "He said his name's—" and just as he turned to gesture toward the bathroom, a blur darted through the door and smacked Todd in the head with a clothes iron.

Teeth went everywhere, clattering dully on the cheap linoleum floor.

Rosa screamed and drew herself up onto the couch so none of the scattering teeth hit her bare feet.

The guy moved closer to her. He wore nothing but a pair of dark blue bikini briefs, at least a couple sizes too small. That was the first thing she noticed. The bulge. Then she looked at his face to see if she recognized him but . . . he didn't have a face. Instead, there was something that looked like a picture of artfully arranged meat he wore like a mask. No eyeholes. No mouth hole. Completely inhuman.

Rosa couldn't help it. She screamed.

The man came toward her, the iron in his hand. Rosa tried to scramble over the back of the couch—that would be the quickest way to the front door—but the man's free hand clasped her around the ankle and yanked her toward him.

As he brought the iron down on her face, Rosa found herself wondering how it was hot enough to make her flesh sizzle when it wasn't even plugged in.

# 6

**K**YLE STEERED WITH ONE HAND while the other contemplatively stroked his nostril hair.

"Your house is even more trashed than the last time I was there," he said.

Tony lit up a cigarette and said, "Yeah, Mom don't like to clean no more. Says she ain't cleanin' unless I stop drinkin'."

"You ever try cleaning?"

"Nah. Ain't for me. No fun."

"But it is fun. Watch this."

Kyle reached down and grabbed a handful of trash and threw it out the window. It was a warm night and he liked driving with the windows down.

He could tell Tony was into it but trying to be cool, as always.

"Huh," Tony said. "Guess I never thought of that."

"Yeah. They never tell you that in school. About how much fun littering is. Everything they tell you in school is wrong. They're just trying to produce boring robots. Go on. Grab some."

"Really?"

Kyle laughed. "Come on, man. Let's live it up. Let's clean this fucking car."

"Okay. Okay. Wait a minute." Tony sifted through the trash on the passenger side until he found a rubber band. He tossed his cigarette out the window, pressed the meat photo against his face, and pulled the rubber band over his head. "I don't want to lose this."

"Right on, man."

Then, like a wild burrowing animal, Tony was grabbing up all the trash from the floorboards and heaving it out the window as Kyle sped through the suburb. They were both laughing. Kyle had never seen Tony laugh like that, although his laughter was somewhat muffled by the mask.

"This feels so good!" Tony cried.

"It's pretty liberating!" Kyle said, going faster and faster.

"Dude, if Mom could drive the house around, there wouldn't be a scrap of trash in it!"

"I tell you what, Tone, if you get this car all cleaned out, we'll go to the store and I'll buy some tires for your house."

Tony opened up the glove compartment and cleared it out with one swipe of his hand. "You fuckin' serious?"

"You bet!"

Tony went into overdrive. Once the passenger side floorboard was empty, he sprang into the back seat. He threw out all the trash he'd been sitting on and got to work on the floorboards in the back.

"You're so much better than Chad." Kyle thought Tony might need some encouraging words. "If you were Chad, I would have had to have taken you to the hospital by now."

Kyle looked in the rearview mirror to see Tony's meat-photo face looking back at him.

"I never liked him," Tony said.

"Me neither!"

Tony kept laughing as he threw handfuls of trash out the window. Kyle watched in the rearview as it swirled around in the empty streets. He'd never thought he could be responsible for doing so much good. He began thinking about how he could replace Chad with Tony. How much better life would be. Kyle could have his wife committed somewhere, probably. She was old and sick. Maybe a nursing home would take her. Then it could just be them. Just the boys. That would be so great. He turned the radio up, cracked a popper, and drove even faster.

# 7

CHAD LAY IN THE BACKYARD listening to an airplane fly overhead in the night sky, not sure why he couldn't see it even though he was pretty sure his head was pointed in the right direction.

"You don't need to see it," a voice said. He couldn't see who said that either. "You already know what it looks like."

He guessed the voice was right about that. How many planes had he seen crawl through the night sky? Actually, probably not that many, if he really thought about it. He hated being outside. Still, he was a bit worried he couldn't see anything even though his eyes were fully open. At least he was pretty sure they were. When he tried to touch his eyelids with his fingertips—something he'd had to do quite a bit to keep his eyes open—he felt, not his eyelids, but a glossy paper-ish . . . something.

He was supposed to do something but he'd already forgotten what that was by the time he made it outside. Once outside, he'd grown too tired to stand and lain in the grass.

"You don't need to use your eyes anymore," the voice said. "I'm here to guide you now."

Then he remembered the meat photo. He liked looking at it and felt sad for a moment that he wouldn't be able to look at it if it was fastened to his head. But if this was what the photo wanted, he would have to think about something else.

Like his eyes. Now that he wasn't using them, they felt incredibly heavy. He wondered if he would ever need them again. The hospital had helped him get rid of his appendix last year and, for a while, he'd felt much lighter. He had no idea why god or whoever would put all these things your body didn't need inside you.

The voice told him to get up. He wanted to resist its direction. Chad would rather lie in the yard. He didn't care that the night air was damp and he felt moist and the dried out and overgrown grass was starting to make him itch. He was just too lazy to move.

"Get up," the voice said. "You have to do some very important things."

Chad jerked to an upright position. He knew the voice would guide him and he didn't need to see. He stumbled through the yard and tripped a few times. He tripped over the curb when his feet met the pavement. The voice guided him down the street, rambling about sacrifice and something wonderful waiting for him on the next level.

# 8

**R**ICHARD JOHNSON WAS SO HAPPY his parents had named him Richard Johnson. It was like they had the foresight to name him Dick Dick or Cock Cock. Maybe they had known when he was born, while he lay naked and covered in afterbirth, that his cock would be famous someday.

The camera flashed and brought Richard back from his daydreaming. He looked at the computer screen to see the composition of the photo: a shot of him from the waist down, naked, with one leg lifted and placed on a simple but artfully modern chair, with an empty pig's intestine encasing his dick and hanging to the floor, an oversized sausage protruding from his anus, and stacks of beautiful meat arranged around his feet. As he looked at the photo, he wondered if he should turn his hips a little to expose more of the sausage in his anus without losing the focus on his cock.

*No*, he thought. *No one visits my OnlyFans to see my anus. They want a shot of this beautiful cock.*

The camera flashed again. The timer was still going and would continue to snap a photo every ten seconds until he shut it off. He had an idea.

He moved some of the meat at his feet around and repositioned himself so his ass was facing the camera before bending over. The intestines pulled and slid down his cock, causing him to become partially erect. Richard readjusted the meat casing. He pushed the base of his cock to force it down so it would show up in the photo. The oversized sausage slipped from his ass and landed in the pile of meat on the floor. The camera flash went off again.

"Goddammit," he cursed.

Richard looked between his legs at the computer screen and it took a few seconds for him to register what he was seeing. The photo wasn't bad, even with the sausage suspended in midair, his anus gaping from its escape, but there was someone standing in the background with a mask on. He lifted his head to find the intruder.

A smallish and overweight woman stood to his left, wearing a pretty tasteful shot of meat on her face, even though it wasn't one of Richard's photos, and she held an enormous piece of meat by the bone protruding from it. Richard didn't have time to react as the woman lifted the meat and brought it crashing down on his head but his last thought was, *Please don't hurt my beautiful cock.*

# 9

AGNES HAD JUST FINISHED MASTURBATING with an old empty Coke bottle she'd found on the bedside table. It was full of spent cigarette butts but she didn't care. She really wished it had been full so she could've drunk it. After Chad had taken the photo, she'd felt antsy and couldn't stop thinking about it, the way the meat glistened and appeared to bulge. It made her hungry in more than one way.

She was thirsty and hungry but had gotten bored after screaming for Chad to bring her some more Munch. She was regretting telling the worthless piece of shit to burn the photo. She was really hungry and, if she had the photo, she could at least look at it and dream of days gone by when she'd eaten. It had been at least an hour since the last time she'd had some Munch. Remembering all that meat had made her wet, and since Kyle could hardly get it up anymore, she'd decided the Coke bottle would be a better option than waiting for him to come home.

Agnes screamed for Chad some more. She screamed for Kyle. She screamed for some more Munch but knew everyone in the family was worthless and she would have to get some more on her own. But more than the Munch, she wanted that fucking photo of meat. She needed it. Something in her compelled her to go after it.

She rolled around on the bed until she made it to the edge. The need for food, and the photo, gave her a new energy and she was able to sit up, something she hadn't been able to do in ages. Agnes was sweaty and breathing heavily when she reached for her two dusty canes. She rocked back and forth a few times and, using the canes as leverage, was able to get to her feet. She felt dizzy but was filled with an unexplainable power to keep going.

Agnes bellowed, "Meat photo!" before starting her journey to find it.

# 10

KYLE PARKED THE CAR OUTSIDE the dark nursing home and killed the engine. The only lights on were in the lobby and the parking lot was dimly lit by the building sign.

Tony had cleaned all the trash from the car and sat silently in the passenger seat, smoking a cigarette by slipping it under the meat photo mask.

"What the fuck are we doin' here?" Tony flipped the cigarette butt out the car window.

"Well," Kyle said, "weren't we going to fuck some shit up?"

"You were gonna buy me some tires."

"I will. But I thought we could make a quick stop before getting the tires. All these old fucks, I hate old people. That's why I like hangin' out with you, Tone. You're young and full of energy. Man, if I make it to this age, do me a favor. Fuckin' kill me." Kyle stroked his nose hair before gesturing toward the nursing home. "Look at them." He looked at the clock on the dash. "It's only eleven o'clock and they're all in bed—"

The sound and smell of spray paint permeated the car as Tony filled the wet and crusty fast-food sack he'd found when tossing trash out the window.

"Fuck yeah," Kyle said. "Give me a hit of that."

After hitting the bag, Kyle felt deeply relaxed. He leaned his seat back, a large smile spreading across his face. The pulsing buzz filling his head was soothing.

"Good shit," he said.

"I guess," Tony said. "Krylon's better but this was all I could afford. Found it at the Dollar General."

"It works."

"I got time to smoke?"

"We got all the time in the world."

Tony lit up a cigarette.

"Not like those people." Kyle gestured toward the old folks' home. "Their days are numbered."

"What do you think they're doing in there?" Tony said.

"Probably fucking. Must be a pretty sweet life. They don't have to think about anything. People just wheel 'em around and when they go back to their rooms, it's just an endless sea of cock and pussy."

"Cock. And. Pussy."

"Hell yeah." Kyle's eyes glittered as he stared toward the home. He knew Tony was feeling it too. "I just want to tell you how cool you are, Tone. How much more fun than Chad you are. Last summer, I tried to take him babe watching at the public pool. You know what happened?"

"He pull it out in front of everybody?"

Kyle smiled and laughed a little. "I wish. Stupid little fucker broke out in a rash."

"Everyone at school thinks there's something wrong with him."

"You ever wonder . . ." Kyle trailed off, absently stroking his nostril hairs.

"Wonder what?"

"You ever wonder if your mom would notice if we replaced you with Chad?"

"I don't know. She barely notices me."

"Maybe we'll try it sometime."

"I could probably just move in with you. We could keep Chad in a cage in the basement."

Kyle hit the bag again and pointed at Tony. "I like the way you think." Then, after a few more seconds, he said, "My wife would never go for it though. I tried to make him stay in the shed out back but she made me let him in. She doesn't like him either, so I don't know what the big deal is. She kept worrying someone would call

CPS or something."

"Whoa, check it out," Tony said.

A person wandered out of the nursing home. The person was nude but so old and fat Kyle couldn't tell if it was a man or a woman. They wore a meat photo as a mask.

"That's just like mine," Tony said.

"Maybe not exactly," Kyle said. "Not all photos of meat are the same."

"You should get one for yourself."

"You think?"

"Definitely. It'd be so cool. Like we were in the same gang or something."

"You ready to fuck some shit up?"

"Absolutely." Tony flicked his cigarette out the window.

They got out of the car. It wasn't the first time they'd done this. Kyle approached the elderly obese person and shoved them down. When they hit the ground, their stomach lifted and Kyle could finally see that it was a man. The man didn't say anything. Kyle bent down and stripped the mask off him, putting it on his face.

"How do I look?" he asked Tony.

"I don't know, man. I can't see anything."

"Let's go terrorize some grannies."

"Fuck yeah."

They opened the front door and walked in. The receptionist at the front desk, upon seeing them, began screaming.

# 11

**D**EREK FOSBERG HAD BEEN WORKING out for the past three days straight. His muscles felt rock hard and his head felt like it was going to explode. He felt amazing. It wasn't that he'd intended to work out for three straight days. He'd forgotten which apartment he lived in and was too embarrassed to ask the building manager. Not that they'd be in the office at this hour anyway. He'd just have to keep going until the morning at least. He felt up to it, although he was a little worried that if his muscles got any bigger or harder, they'd rip out of his skin. As he worked the kettle bell, he thought about what it would be like to have muscles on the outside of your body. Pretty fucking cool, he was sure.

He looked at himself in the wall of mirrors. Veins he didn't even know he possessed bulged from his neck and arms.

Then he saw a figure enter the gym. It was a man wearing bikini briefs with Merry Christmas written over his cock and something over his face.

*What the fuck?*

He waited for the guy to pick up some weights or something, but he just stood there with his head pointed in Derek's direction. Derek didn't know if the man could see him or not because there weren't

24

any eyeholes in the mask.

Derek felt bothered and indestructible. This dude was really pissing him off. He wasn't sure if the guy was some sort of pervert or if he thought this was a place he could go cruising. He dropped the kettle bell onto the rubberized floor to turn and confront the intruder. His muscles were so big and stiff it was hard to move. Derek felt like an indestructible wall.

"What the fuck you lookin' at, freak?"

The man continued to keep his head pointed in Derek's general direction. As Derek moved closer to him, he saw that the thing on his face was a photo of meat. Artfully arranged, beautifully photographed meat. He'd never seen anything like it. At first he thought the guy was here to creep him out or maybe even hurt him, but now he wasn't so sure.

"You gonna say somethin' or you want me to rip you in half?" Derek didn't even know why he said this. He didn't want to rip this guy in half. Maybe this guy was just here to watch him work out.

"Oh, I get it," Derek said. He was pretty sure his voice had grown deeper since he'd started working out. He figured his balls had probably grown, just like his muscles. "You like to watch, huh?"

The man nodded his head.

"Sure thing, buddy. You want a show, you got it."

Derek couldn't forget his reason for bulking up. He wanted people to watch him. One day, he hoped he could stroll out onto a stage in front of a packed room and turn and flex his awesome muscles while everyone watched in envy and resentment.

He went to the barbells and loaded one of them with weights. He'd never tried to deadlift this much weight before. He didn't even know how many pounds he'd put on there, but it looked impressive. And he was sure he could do it.

"You ain't never seen anything like this," he said.

He got into position and bent to wrap his hands around the textured bar. He saw himself lifting it. He saw himself lifting it so powerfully that he launched the bar and all the weights up through the ceiling. He had to do it in one clean jerk or it would look clumsy and amateurish. He braced his knees into position and gave a jerk.

What followed was a total mess.

One of his eyes popped out of his head. A loud sound came from his ass and he was momentarily afraid he'd shit himself but a glance at the mirrors confirmed that it was much worse. His bowels trailed from the legs of his shorts. He wasn't to be deterred, however. He continued straining with the bar. It felt like all of his insides were now sliding out of his ass. He watched a vein in his neck swell before it exploded, coating the mirror in a spray of red. He could feel the skin peeling off his palms. He was starting to lose consciousness.

Before everything turned black, he was pretty sure he heard the man in the meat photo mask clapping.

# 12

**T**HE NEXT THING CHAD KNEW, he stood in front of a dirty front door on a porch covered in trash. He no longer needed his eyes to know this. The mask made him aware of everything around him.

"Tony! That you?!" a shrill voice called from inside.

Chad had to think about it. Was he Tony? Had someone changed his name?

The door swung open and Chad was blasted with the smell of cigarette smoke and a million other putrid scents lurking beneath it.

"I told you not to wear that damn thing no more." The woman reached for the mask but quickly brought her hand away. "Take it off. I'm not gonna let you bite me again."

Chad barely knew what was happening. Why was he here? He turned to walk away.

"Where you goin'?" the woman said. "Didn't you bring back no trash?"

Chad didn't know. He turned back around. It felt like the world was swimming around him. He reached into his pockets and felt what were probably crumpled bags of Munch. He pulled them out and handed them to the woman.

She took them from him and tossed them back into the house.

"I'm so proud of you," she said.

No one had ever said this to him before. He didn't know what he was supposed to do.

"Could at least say thanks, you little shit."

He raised a hand to touch the mask. It was comforting. It was telling him to go into the house and, before he knew it, he was pushing his way into the hoard. He'd never felt anything like it. The claustrophobia of everything piled up around him as he made his way down the narrow goat path was revelatory, intoxicating.

"Tony, what's wrong with you?" the woman said from behind him.

Chad was terrified of water but he imagined he was in a pool filled with trash. It wasn't completely dry. Moist. That was the word he was looking for. It felt like he was swimming in a moist pool of trash and he loved it. The mask told him what to do and he continued exploring his new world, looking for a portal that would take him to the next level. He tripped and fell on what he thought might've been a cat's carcass. It was dried out and the skin was stretched over its bones. It could've been an opossum. Either way it smelled bad and he was compelled to keep going. He knew the portal was somewhere within the house.

He moved through the wet garbage until his mind spotted a green door streaked with fuzzy black mold. Chad knew it would take him to the next level. He knocked over the stacks of moist magazines sitting in front of the door.

"Goddammit, Tony! Where the hell ya goin'?" She ripped open a bag of Munch and began devouring handfuls.

Chad ignored the woman, grabbed the door knob, and pulled on the door. It resisted being opened. The bottom of the door scraped up a thick layer of brown sludge on the floor, spotted with mouse turds. He had to yank on it a few times, toppling more trash stacked near it, before it revealed the dark throat of the basement stairs.

Her mouth full, the woman said, "Now I done told you . . ." The woman stomped toward him, the floor sinking and threatening to cave in as she neared him, the motion causing a large pile of trash stacked to the ceiling to come crashing down on her and blocking the way back out of the house.

Chad didn't care that the path to the front door was now gone. The voice told him he was going in the right direction. He fumbled around until he found a light switch and flipped it. A single bulb illuminated the murk below. The steps were filled with trash and someone had stomped on the stuff enough to flatten a spot on every stair so he could at least make his way down them. He'd only made it a few steps before hearing something that made him stop.

*Clunk.*

He stared at what lay in the basement. Water. It scared him. The smell nauseated him. Stacks of boxes and junk store items were submerged in five feet of water. A few rubber totes floated on the water and knocked together. *Clunk.* Chad saw what he thought was a turd float by. His skin crawled at the sight of the water.

The voice said, "It's time to take it to the next level."

Chad knew what he had to do. He cannonballed into the fetid basement water.

# 13

MRS. STEVENSON HAD TAKEN AN interest in the *Don Tross Meat Painting Show* after the death of her husband ten years ago. Don Tross was a soft-spoken man who painted on PBS. He had a reverse mohawk, which was a bit unusual for such an old fellow, but that didn't matter to Mrs. Stevenson. She tuned in every day.

At first she only watched him during the afternoon to lull her into a nap. His hushed voice was comforting after all those years of Mr. Stevenson screaming at her to get off her fucking ass and fix him something to eat. He was screaming at her to bring him five ice cream sandwiches when he had his heart attack. Then he was screaming at her to call 911. And then he screamed at her to burn in hell for sitting there and watching him clutch his chest. Eventually he turned red, then purple, then passed out and died. Whenever she thought about her husband like that she got aroused. But thinking about his screaming would give her palpitations and listening to Don Tross would always soothe her.

After a year of afternoon naps Mrs. Stevenson started watching the *Don Tross Meat Painting Show*. Not only did Don Tross paint a picture of meat every day, he painted the same picture of meat every day.

30

It was predictable, but yet, each show was a different filming, so each painting was the same but different. Six months after watching Don Tross she started to paint along with him, filling her house with 2,218 paintings of the same painting he did every weekday. She stacked them against the walls of the house she and her husband shared for forty-three years before he finally died and left the house and all the peace and quiet to her. She'd discovered the joys of both watching the show so she could nap and taping the show each day on the same VHS, recording over the previous day's show so she could watch it at night and paint before going to bed.

She'd stripped down to her yellowed granny panties and Playtex bra, preparing to watch the *Don Tross Meat Painting Show* and paint along. She preferred to be in her underwear for the painting. A year ago, Mrs. Stevenson had developed a tremor in her painting hand. It had grown steadily worse and now she made a bit of a mess of her paintings and herself as she followed along with Don Tross. It was just easier to strip down, shower, and turn in afterward if she painted in her underwear.

Mrs. Stevenson hit the play button on the VCR and the VHS squealed to life. The tape, having seen its better days, made a horrid noise as it played, and Mrs. Stevenson turned the TV volume up as far as it would go before preemptively prepping her canvas. She knew if she didn't start before Don Tross she would never finish the painting before she got too tired.

The opening credits started and she was ready. She lost herself in the meat. The way it glistened. The way it was artfully arranged. She was becoming one with the construction of the meat in the painting when someone pounded on her front door.

"Who in sandhill . . ."

*BANG! BANG! BANG!*

She thought she would ignore it. It was probably the junkies next door. They were forever banging on people's doors, all times of the night, wanting a cigarette.

"I don't smoke!" she yelled. Her tremor got worse when she was angry and she messed up her painting.

*BANG! BANG! BANG!*

"Oh for crying out loud!"

She threw her paint brush on the floor and hit pause on the tape before stomping as fast as an old lady could toward the door. Whoever it was was gonna get an eyeful of old flesh and she didn't give a damn.

Mrs. Stevenson threw open the door to find an overweight woman sweating and panting on her front step. She thought she recognized the woman but she couldn't be sure. Maybe a neighbor. Yeah, she was sure she'd seen the woman a couple of times as her husband hoisted her into their car, using a wheelbarrow to move her from the house to the car and back.

Before Mrs. Stevenson could ask what in the hell the woman wanted, the woman bellowed, "Meat photo!" and charged her, knocking her to the floor and into a stack of her precious paintings.

The intruder grabbed one of her paintings, stared at it for a brief moment, and dropped to her knees by Mrs. Stevenson. The woman clutched the painting to her chest and screamed in Mrs. Stevenson's face, "Meat photo!" before lifting the painting and bringing it down on Mrs. Stevenson's head.

The woman continued to beat Mrs. Stevenson with her own painting, repeatedly screaming. The woman finally collapsed on the floor and spotted the paint brush Mrs. Stevenson had dropped. She wrapped her thick fingers around the paintbrush, and while Mrs. Stevenson moaned on the floor, she rammed the handle of the brush into the old woman's eye before grabbing another undamaged painting from the ones scattered on the floor and darting out the door.

# 14

A LITTLE WHILE LATER, KYLE AND Tony came running out of the nursing home. Tony was laughing and full of energy. Kyle really admired his enthusiasm. When he was around Tony, it was almost like Chad didn't exist. Almost.

Sometime during their time in the nursing home, they'd lost all their clothes except their shoes and underwear. They didn't stop running until they got to the car.

"All right," Kyle said, slightly winded. "High five!"

Tony smacked Kyle's palm, coughed, and said, "I need a smoke."

"Oh, man," Kyle said. "Hope you didn't leave them in your clothes."

"Got 'em right here." Tony gestured down to the waistband of his underwear.

"Right on," Kyle said.

They leaned back against the car.

"Do we need to worry about the cops showing up?"

"Are you kidding?" Kyle reached up to stroke his nostril hair but the meat photo covered it up. Instead, he stroked the surface of the photo, imagining the glistening meat artfully arranged therein. "Meat photo," he whispered.

"Huh?" Tony said.

"What I meant was . . . we showed those old fucks the time of their lives tonight."

"I guess," Tony said. "I think I broke Edith's hip."

"She can get a new one. All those old people, their parts are pretty much replaceable."

Tony took a deep drag of his cigarette and said, "Man, I don't want this night to ever end," as he exhaled a plume of smoke.

"Stick with me and it could last forever."

Kyle didn't even know if this was true. This time wasn't like any other time he and Tony had ever come to the nursing home. Usually they went in through the back door while the receptionist was out front having a smoke. Then they would go around to the various rooms and tell the residents they were some relative who the person would typically have absolutely no recollection of. Then they would proceed to tell the resident what an awful person they were, making up things that had never happened. But tonight, as soon as the receptionist passed out from screaming so much, loud dance music came from seemingly everywhere. Kyle felt like they had lost their clothes around then. A quick glance into the residents' rooms revealed that none of them were there.

They followed the source of the music until they reached the cafeteria. The usual harsh fluorescent lighting was replaced with a flashing, multi-colored strobe light. The elderly stood around, most of them nude, all of them wearing meat photos. A thick vapor roiled around the room and this put Kyle into an immediate party mood. Some of the elderly were attempting to dance but none of them were doing it particularly well. One of them—Beverly, if Kyle remembered correctly—was hunched over her walker murmuring, "Meat photo."

An old guy named Frank pointed at them and said, "Hey, they're one of us now."

As if on cue, Kyle and Tony slid to the middle of the floor and showed the elderly how to dance. They kept going until they worked up a massive sweat and most of the elderly had collapsed onto the floor. Kyle continued dancing in the middle of the floor, occasionally having to nudge an old person out of the way with his foot, while Tony grinded on some of the finer old folks. Kyle didn't know how long they kept it up, through two or three songs at least. And the songs seemed exceptionally long. When he got tired and Tony doubled over with a coughing fit, he figured it was probably time to go.

"It smells like shit and death in here!" he called to Tony.

"Yeah!" Tony called back. "I love it!"

"Let's beat it."

"Right on, man!" Tony yanked his underwear down and began masturbating furiously.

"Whoa, dude! I didn't mean that. Let's get the fuck outta here."

Tony, always too cool to be embarrassed, pulled his underwear back up and followed Kyle out of the building.

Now, as Tony finished his cigarette and tossed it out into the parking lot, Kyle said, "You ready to go see about getting some tires for that house."

"Fuck yeah," Tony said.

# 15

"**WHAT THE HELL ARE YOU DOING** in there?!" Bob's wife, Kendra, yelled from the living room.

"Leave me alone!" he shouted. "I'm just trying to take a come!"

"Make sure you let me see it this time! Don't flush it away like last time! I ain't never been with a guy who can't come at least a half a cup. I gotta see if you measure up."

Bob knew he could never produce a half-cup of semen. He'd heard all about Kendra's previous lovers, how copious their discharges were. He decided he couldn't even compete. He knew Kendra would never love him for who he was, and that was okay. He was only with Kendra because she was the best-looking woman he'd ever dated. He was surprised when she'd said yes after asking her to marry him on only their second date. That was only a couple of weeks ago. No, he couldn't give her the volume she wanted, so he had another idea.

He furiously worked his penis, staring at his beady eyes and the warts covering his shaved head in the bathroom mirror. He squeezed more tightly than he ever had and pulled harder and harder. He snarled under his breath, "Meat photo. Meat photo. Meat photo." He uttered those words faster and faster as he increased his rhythm.

The meat photo seemed to be Kendra's latest obsession. She'd found it in her underwear drawer shortly after they'd come back from the honeymoon at the Holiday Inn the next town over. She'd been virtually unable to look at him ever since. He wondered what the meat photo had that he didn't but the answer was obvious. All that red and glistening meat, lightly marbled with fat. After gazing into its depths a few times, he felt stupid for thinking he'd ever compare to it.

He continued jerking off, muttering those magic words, when Kendra made a sound that almost sounded like she was having an orgasm before being quickly replaced with blood-curdling shrieks. Maybe he should have been concerned but he was so close to finishing.

When he finished, he knew he would be perfect for her.

He heard someone fidgeting with the doorknob. Kendra, probably. Of course it was Kendra. Who else could it be?

"Not now!" he shouted. "Oh god, I'm doing it! I'm coming!!!"

And just as the first paltry load of semen shot from his cock, he gave a mighty yank and ripped the skin off. It was still warm in his hand when the door burst open and someone wearing that meat photo as a mask stood in the doorway.

The figure in the doorway seemed momentarily distracted by Bob's skinned penis and the blooms of bright red blood blossoming on the bathroom tiles.

Before the knife took his eyes, Bob was able to glance down and witness his creation. It was a raw, glistening red tube. Perfection. Kendra would have been so happy, he thought before thinking, "Meat photo," and surrendering to death.

# 16

AGNES DIDN'T KNOW WHERE SHE was. A bike path of some kind. Illuminated by the moonlight, it was littered with trash and more organs than she thought should be on the bike path. True, it had been years since she'd even left her house, so maybe that was just how things were now. Ever since she'd made it to her feet she'd felt invigorated. Each step made her feel more powerful than the last. She didn't even need her canes anymore and had discarded them in the yard on her way to the bike path. She picked through some of the trash, hoping with everything she had that one of the scraps of paper would turn out to be her sought-after meat photo. She didn't know why she'd asked Chad to get rid of it. She didn't know why she thought Chad would ever be *able* to get rid of it. She knew there was no way he'd have the ambition to burn it. She didn't know where Chad had gotten off to and, eventually, as she wandered farther along the path, she wasn't even sure if she knew who Chad was, her child or just some kid who hung out there a lot. She didn't remember giving birth to anyone. She wrote it off to the Munch. She'd had at least three bags today and sometimes it made her do weird things. She knew Kyle really liked hanging out with boys. Said he was robbed of it when he was their age because his folks mostly kept him locked in a cellar when he wasn't working at the paper factory.

Eventually, Agnes had an idea. She found an old plastic bag from a local pharmacy plastered to a tree along the bike path. The next organ she came to—she had no idea what it was because she'd never paid attention in school—she lifted it up from the ground and dropped it into her bag. With each organ she picked up she felt a lightening in her step. She decided she wasn't going to go home until the bag was absolutely stuffed with organs. Then she wouldn't even need that stupid old meat photo. She could just look into her magic bag. Lose herself in it. Just to give herself a glimpse of the pleasures it contained, she plunged her hand into the bag and fondled the organs. She pulled the bag up to her face and took a deep breath.

"Meat photo," she said to it. Had she snapped the meat photo she'd asked Chad to get rid of? She couldn't remember. She couldn't remember ever artfully arranging meat before taking a photo of it. Surely, if she had, she would remember. One does not forget a thing like that. Not only did the Munch make her sometimes act in strange ways but, because she'd used it so habitually for so long, she was pretty sure it was starting to affect her memory. Why couldn't she have been the photographer who'd taken the meat photo?

The more organs she found and stuffed in the bag, the less it mattered. Soon there would be another meat photo or, better yet, the real thing. Why did she need a photo of artfully arranged meat to stroke and pleasure herself to when she could have the real thing? Kyle never slept in bed with her anymore. She could fill his side of the bed with artfully arranged meat. She could stroke it whenever. Feel it. Feel the meat, not just the glossy surface of some old photo. She could smell it while she masturbated. Already she was thinking about the powerful climax that would give her.

She placed another organ in the bag. Pretty sure this one was some kind of heart. She felt herself grow slightly wet between the legs and she couldn't wait to get home with her new found treasure.

Sometimes the world could be a pretty fantastic place.

# 17

JESSICA SCREAMED FROM HER BED, "Goddammit! Would you kids shut the fuck up and go to bed already?!"

The youngest, James, only five years old, replied, "Fuck you, Mom!"

"Yeah," Don, two years older, added, "Fuck you! We'll do whatever we want! Jus' try and stop us!"

"You little shits!" Jessica yelled. "I should've aborted both of ya! I'd come out and whoop both yer asses but I'm trying to watch my shows! If you make me get out of this bed after I've worked a double shift I'm gonna murder both of ya! Ya hear me! I'll cut both yer peckers off!"

The kids laughed and continued to squabble over whatever they'd been fighting about since Jessica got home. She didn't give a shit what they were fighting about. She'd spent sixteen hours on her swollen feet behind the counter at Arby's, because they had the meats. Meat was all Jessica could think about anymore. She saw it all day at work and she just couldn't get enough of it. She liked to artfully arrange the meat on trays before the cooks fried it up to serve to a bunch of ungrateful customers. And the cooks didn't give a shit either. She'd set the trays down gingerly to not disturb her creations but the cooks never noticed. They'd just plunge their grubby little hands into her masterpieces and slap them on the grill.

The rage that built up within Jessica every day nearly boiled over until she discovered MeatTV, a free online streaming channel. Well, it was free if you wanted to watch commercials. For $9.99 a month you could get MeatTV Premium, which offered all the MeatTV you could ever want without the interruptions of antidepressant commercials. It was like the people who ran MeatTV thought all their viewers needed to be medicated. Jessica knew she didn't need to be medicated. MeatTV was her medication. She found that lying in bed after work, while still wearing her work uniform permeated with the stench of meat, and watching endless videos of meat was all she ever wanted out of life.

Jessica focused on her tablet as the camera panned over piles and piles of glistening meat. Although she was enjoying the twenty-four hours of meat, the way the camera person chose to shoot the meat was downright wrong.

"Who the fuck arranged this meat?" she murmured under her breath. She knew that if she had arranged the mountain of meat they were showing, the channel would get millions more views. She'd have to remember to look and see if there was any way to contact the producers. She thought if she arranged some meat, filmed it with her phone, and sent it to MeatTV, they'd probably pay her millions of dollars to film segments for their channel.

One of the kids shouted, "Meat photo!"

Jessica growled and then shouted, "Shut the fuck up, you assholes!" The force of her shouting caused her to go into a coughing fit and she dropped the tablet on the bed. She continued to cough so hard it shook the bed and the tablet slid to the floor. Jessica scrambled to catch the device but wasn't quick enough and her heart skipped a beat as she heard the sickening crack when the tablet hit the hardwood floor.

"No no no no no." She flopped around on the bed until she was able to sit on its edge. Her stomach dropped when she looked down to see the tablet's screen had broken and the only picture behind the spiderweb of glass was white. "Fuck! Fuck! Fuck!" She scooped the tablet up, hoping the white screen was a glitch and the video would come back on soon. It didn't. She smacked the tablet on the side with her hand but still nothing.

A loud crash came from the living room. It sounded like a bomb and shook the entire house.

"You little motherfuckers! I'm gonna kill both of you! You ruined my tablet!"

She growled as she rose from the bed and stomped toward the living room. Jessica didn't know what she was expecting to find when she made it there but she knew she was going to have to come up with an excuse as to why she'd eviscerated her two children and carefully arranged their insides on plates when the police finally arrived.

Jessica stopped short when she entered the living room as she took in the scene. The floor to ceiling entertainment center had been flipped over. Don stood on the other side of the destroyed furniture, naked, breathing heavily, and wearing a beautiful photo of meat on his face. Jessica noticed something twitch on the ground before going still and spotted two tiny feet protruding from under the entertainment center.

She turned her attention back to Don and calmly said, "You little cunt goblin. Yer gonna spend the rest of your life locked up in a loony bin." She began to laugh.

"Meat photo!" Don screamed. He clambered over the rubble and rushed toward her.

Something about the ferocity of his scream scared Jessica. Hell, the fact he'd killed his brother should have been terrifying but Jessica knew she outweighed Don and could probably snap his neck easily, something she'd fantasized about doing since the day he was born.

"Meat photo! Meat photo! Meat photo!"

Jessica turned to run back to her room just as Don launched himself onto her back. He wrapped his legs around her waist and began to claw at her face.

She screamed in pain and ran into the bathroom instead of her bedroom. Her thoughts were a racing mess of chaos. She was a wild animal in fight-or-flight mode and she was choosing to do both. She swung her body wildly, trying to shake the boy off, but failed. She turned and rammed her back into the bathroom wall, hoping to knock him off or knock the air out of him, but instead he ripped off one of her ears. The pain was excruciating and she fell onto her hands and knees, gripping the open wound where her ear once was.

The boy jumped off her. She knew he was fumbling with something behind the toilet but all she could focus on was the horrendous pain on the side of her head. She wailed as something hit her hard in the taint and launched her forward. Her head slammed into the bathtub and the world spun. She groggily turned her head.

"Meat photo!"

Don held a plunger against his tiny penis, the handle of the tool pointed directly at her behind. He backed up against the wall, aimed the handle of the plunger at her ass, and charged at her.

"Meat photo!"

Jessica focused on the beautiful photo of meat as the handle of the plunger ripped the pants of her Arby's uniform, ripped her panties, and plunged deep into her anus, perforating her colon, and harpooning her insides.

# 18

"**W**HAT KIND OF TIRES ARE ya gonna buy me?" Tony said.

"I don't know," Kyle said. "Probably used ones. Maybe some tractor tires. Whatever we can get at Walmart. It's the only thing open this time of night."

"Why don't we just steal some?"

"That's why I like you, Tony." Kyle stroked the meat photo, finding it more soothing than his nose hair. "You're so much smarter than Chad. I really wish you were my son. Hey, when we get done picking up the tires do you wanna go to a strip club?"

"Maybe."

"Maybe? Thought you might want to see some tits."

"Saw some tits already at the old folks' home. I want to see some pictures of meat."

"What if we go back to the nursing home and steal some of the meat photos from the gross old people and take them to a strip club and pay the strippers to wear them? That'd be cool."

"I don't know. Seems contrived." Tony pulled a cigarette from his pack.

"I guess Tony's an art critic now."

He shrugged and stuck the cigarette in his mouth. Only . . . the mask. It was like the meat photo had become a part of Tony's face, opening to easily accept the cigarette. Tony really was a special boy.

"Don't worry, dude. You're still way better than Chad. Let's go get those fuckin' tires. You know how to drive a tractor?"

"I can figure it out."

"I bet you can."

Kyle drove them to Walmart.

As soon as they walked through the automatic doors, the ancient greeter said, "You can't come in without—" He stopped at seeing the meat photos on their faces. "Ah, I know exactly what you're looking for. Follow me."

Tony and Kyle looked at each other and shrugged. Tony stroked his mask and thought he could almost *feel* the glistening meats in the photo.

"I'm not gonna lie," Kyle said. "I'm a little hard right now." He didn't even know why he said it. Wearing only his underwear, it should have been plain for anyone to see.

Tony and Kyle followed the old man through the mostly deserted store. The old man moved so slowly, Kyle wanted to push him out of the way and go straight to the automotive section. Maybe the old man knew that's what they were here for. Maybe that's where he was taking them. But, no, after what felt like half an hour, Kyle and Tony were standing in front of the meat section—a whole wall of it. Every kind of meat, nearly as far as the eye could see.

"Help yourself. It's all free." The old man gave them a knowing wink and pulled something out of his pocket. He unfolded it and looked proudly up at Kyle. It was a photo of meat. "I have a couple more at home but this place doesn't pay me much so I have to wait 'til I get paid before I buy another one."

"You shouldn't crumple it up like that," Kyle said. "These things are gonna be worth big money someday. And you should put it on. Be proud of who you are."

The old man looked confused and rummaged through his pockets. He held the meat photo up to his face.

"Oh, yeah, you need some help," Kyle said. He found a staple gun on an abandoned service cart and approached the old man. "Hold still." He pressed the staple gun against the meat photo and fired two staples into the guy's forehead. The meat photo radiated a kind of ecstasy Kyle was certain reflected how the old man felt.

"Where you keep the tractor tires?" Tony said like he wasn't even interested in the wall of meat.

"I don't think we sell tractor tires," the old man said. "Maybe in your more rural Walmarts but, no, not here."

"Fuck this shit," Tony said, pulling out a cigarette and lighting up. "I'm gonna burn this place to the fuckin' ground."

"I'd better go get a fire extinguisher," the old man said and turned to walk away.

"I don't think he's really on Team Meat at all," Kyle said. "He's just doing it for the attention."

"What are we gonna do?"

Kyle, staring at the wall of meat, said, "You think we can make tires from meat?"

Tony shrugged. "Probably. I think we can do pretty much anything."

"All right. Let's load up."

"Want me to get a cart?"

"I don't like pushing carts."

"Yeah. Me either. Fuck carts." This gave Tony pause. "But . . . carts have wheels. Every cart has like four wheels, at least."

"You thinking what I'm thinking?"

"It's gonna be a lot of work. Let me finish my smoke and then I'll be ready."

Kyle and Tony each stroked the meat while Tony smoked. Kyle found himself dissatisfied with the plastic shrink wrapping and had to tear a pack open to feel a raw leg of lamb.

# 19

"**T**ONY! DON'T MAKE ME COME down there!"

Claire Anthony had never seen Tony act this way. Usually he was out running around with weird older men or jerking off in his bedroom. He'd never taken an interest in the basement before. And now he was down there exploring it like Christopher fucking Columbus. She didn't know how he could take it. True, some of what was down there was water, but most of it was from the toilets. They'd kept backing up until Claire's fifth husband had fixed them. It wasn't until one of her lovers told her the toilets just emptied straight into the basement that she realized how Husband Five had "fixed" the problem. She hadn't noticed the smell because nothing could really overpower the stench of her hoard.

One thing was for sure: she wasn't going to go down there after him. In fact, she hoped he stayed down there so long he picked up some irreversible illness from all the bacteria. Then she could finally be alone with her hoard. She knew it would forever be a work in progress but there was still so much more she could do with it. It had so much potential. She hadn't really expanded the outside as much as she would've liked yet. Hadn't even received a complaint from the city, as much as she tried. She had a lot of work to do. She figured the junk needed to be at least five feet tall before someone complained.

She began looking for her laptop so she could order an abundance of low-priced items from Amazon. She liked when you could just buy a big box of random things. She didn't care what they were. They all had their place in the hoard.

She shifted some piles of trash out of the way roughly where she thought her laptop should be. She heard Tony down there splashing around in the basement. Maybe he was coughing and gagging or maybe that was just her wishful thinking.

She bent down over her immense girth to move a photo of meat out of the way. It was probably lying on her laptop. She didn't know where all these photos of meat came from. Of course, she would never think about throwing them away, but she couldn't recall ever buying any of them. Maybe they'd come in from one of the estate-sale purchases she'd made.

She couldn't pick up the photo. It wouldn't move. Then she realized it was attached to a person. The person was mostly obscured by trash so she couldn't tell if it was a man or a woman.

She screamed in fright and the figure shoved a piece of her hoard in her mouth to silence her. The figure wrestled her to the floor and Claire now felt certain it was a man. They were too big and strong not to be.

Now she was terrified. She kicked her legs, sending the hoard tumbling around them, trying to get away. But every time she screamed, the man took another piece of the hoard and shoved it in her mouth. She wanted to tell him to stop, that everything he put in her mouth was taking away from her life's work, but her throat was soon blocked as more of the hoard was shoved into her mouth.

Before she lost consciousness, she looked into the meat photo, lost herself in it. She had a moment where she wondered if it wasn't Tony, but she could still hear him downstairs.

She wished she could speak so she could tell the killer not to forget about the kid in the basement. He'd always hated her hoard.

# 20

**K**YLE AND TONY TORE OUT of the Walmart parking lot with a trunkful of meat, pulling four shopping carts behind them.

Tony was on his knees in the passenger seat, turned to look out the back window.

"Whoa!" he said. "Look at all the sparks."

"Want to go to Arby's and get a couple Meat Mountains?"

"Hell yeah. I'm starving." Tony uncapped the bottle of cheap vodka he'd swiped from Walmart and took a slug. He handed it over to Kyle, who eagerly accepted it.

They got to the Arby's but it was closed. Kyle threw a rock through the drive-thru window and an alarm started going off. Neither one of them panicked because they knew no one would respond to the alarm. Kyle got out of the car and stood in front of the drive-thru menu, looking at all the succulent meat on it. But it wasn't the same.

"This is all commercial trash," he said.

"Pretty artless," Tony said.

"Arby's ain't got the meats," Kyle said. "We got the meats."

"Let's fix this menu," Tony said.

They busted a hole toward the top of the menu and filled it with meat from the trunk until the display looked like a massive meat photo.

Kyle wished he had a camera or even a phone so he could take a picture of it.

"Now that's art," Tony said, taking a slug of his vodka.

"Team Meat's getting shit done tonight," Kyle said.

"Fuck yeah. Team Meat forever," Tony said.

"I haven't been able to stop thinking about meat photo since the first time I saw it."

"Me either. I think I need more. I wanna wear like five or six, at least."

"You're not tired yet, are you?"

"No way. I'm just getting started."

"Your mom's not gonna be worried about you?"

"Nah. All she thinks about is her hoard. What about your wife?"

"I try not to think about her too much. The Munch has destroyed her brain."

"I hate that shit, man."

"Yeah, it's for the gross normies. Let them have their Munch. We're out here tasting life."

Tony slugged back some more vodka and belched. "Let's go fuck up some more shit."

# 21

**H**ENRY'S CLAIM TO FAME WAS that he was the kid from *Stupid Home Videos* who'd farted in the bathtub and laughed. For some reason this got all the girls wet. That's all he had to tell them when he picked up a woman at a bar. He thought that maybe they thought he had money. He was a minor when the video was filmed and aired. His parents won the ten-thousand-dollar prize and had spent it all on Munch. But he did what he could and showed every girl that came within five feet of him at the bar the video clip.

That's how he'd met Rhonda a few months back. Rhonda was a weathered gal and had a face that made her look like Christopher Walken. Not a young Christopher Walken either. She was wrinkled and leathery. She gave good head though and had nice tits. So it was easy to dismiss her face and stare at her tits while she blew him. It wasn't until he'd shot his load all over her face and she asked for fifty dollars that he discovered she was a sex worker.

That's when everything changed for Henry. *Why bother trying to win a girl over into fucking him when he could just pay them?*

Now he sat in his car, parked at the curb of a street filled with abandoned warehouses, watching a bunch of scantily clad hookers milling about. He wasn't sure what was happening, but they all wore something over their faces and walked in the same direction. They didn't seem to realize he was there, ready and waiting, with his dick in his hand, literally. He stroked himself and watched as another girl walked by with what he thought was a raw roast and he was certain she kept saying "meat photo" as she passed his car.

He spotted a girl who was nude with the exception of heels and whatever all the women were wearing on their faces. The lighting on the street was exceptionally bad.

Henry called to the girl, "Hey! Hey, babe! You wanna make some money?"

The girl stopped and slowly turned to him and murmured something as she began to approach the car. He wasn't sure how she was able to see where she was going because it looked as though whatever she was wearing over her face didn't have any eyeholes. Henry was fine with that though. He thought it must be some sort of fashion trend. And after Rhonda, he wasn't too sure he wanted to see the girl's face.

As the girl approached, he could make out what she was muttering.

"Meat photo. Meat photo. Meat photo."

"What the fuck?" Henry said.

The girl had gotten close enough to his car for him to make out that the mask she was wearing was just a photo of meat. Henry also realized some of the other women on the street had taken notice of him and were headed his way. It was going to be a competition for his baby batter and the thought of women fighting over the fifty dollars he had for one of them to blow him made him rock hard and he stopped pulling on his dick. He didn't want to lose his load before someone sucked him off.

The girl had reached his car, placed her hands on his open window sill, and was bending down to get a look at him when Henry asked, "Hey, baby, you want some of this man meat?" He grabbed the base of his dick and gave it a wag at her.

"Meat photo," she said and reached for his cock.

Henry became lost in the photo of glistening meat the girl was wearing as she grabbed his dick, clamped down like a vice, and began to yank.

"Whoa!" Henry yelled. "Be gentle on my man meat!"

"Meat photo!" she growled and pulled his dick harder.

"Ah! Stop! You're gonna break my dick off!"

"Meat photo!" one of the other girls nearing the car yelled.

A chorus of yells erupted from all the girls. "Meat photo! Meat photo!"

The girl yanking on his dick braced her feet against his car door.

"What are you doing?! Let go!" He clawed at her hand but it was useless.

The girl threw all of her weight backward and Henry's dick was ripped from his body with a sickening squelch. His scream was primal as the girl hit the ground and was replaced by another girl wearing a photo of meat as a mask. Henry couldn't form any words, only screams, as the girls continued to rip him into pieces of meat.

# 22

AGNES HAD DUMPED ALL THE bags of meat she'd collected onto the bed and loosely arranged them into a human shape. Her panties were soaked and she was beyond horny when she climbed up on the bed and straddled the waist of the meat man she'd constructed. The stench was horrible but she couldn't help herself. She grabbed some of the raw meat and began to slide it over her clit. The meat was cold and slimy but it didn't bother her.

She took up a second handful and rubbed it over the nipples of her sagging breasts. "Oh, meat photo," she moaned. The smell of her cunt and the rotting meat mingled into something physical.

The meat she rubbed against her clit was beginning to dry out and she slipped it inside of her before feverishly masturbating. When she climaxed, she screamed, "Meat photo!" before collapsing on top of the pile of meat. She continued to hump the meat, prolonging her orgasm. As she rubbed her cunt against the meat, she spotted a bag of Munch she must have missed. She snatched it up, ripped it open, and began to swallow handfuls of it without even chewing.

Agnes wasn't sure when she fell asleep. She dreamt of a man who had no face. He had a large, poster-sized photo of meat hanging in his house. She didn't know how she knew but she was aware the

54

photo was the original meat photo. It called to her. She knew she had to find it. She had to have it. She had to possess it. And somehow, without ever seeing it, it possessed her. It called to her.

The man in the dream told her she couldn't have the photo but she knew the photo and she were meant to be together, forever.

Agnes woke to the stench and taste of the meat. She'd finished the bag of Munch and had begun to gnaw on the meat in her sleep. The meat squirmed below her. She pushed herself up to find the meat covered in maggots and reeking worse than before. She wasn't sure but she thought she might have been passed out for days.

She couldn't stop thinking about the dream. That photo. It called to her. She had to have it. The thought of it made her want to cry. A voice told her she had to find it. A voice told her exactly where she needed to go to find it. She would do what the voice told her so she could finally be reunited with her meat photo. But before she went, she had to get off with her meat man one last time. Because it just wasn't fair to have a one-night stand with a perfectly arranged man of meat.

# 23

CHAD FLOPPED AROUND IN WATER, looking for the next level. The smell of the water was almost too much to bear but the voice assured him he would be rewarded. He reached the end of the water and was stopped by something. He traveled around the perimeter of the basement, sloshing through the chin-high water, but there seemed to be some kind of a force field between him and the next level. Only, it wasn't really a force field, because he could see it, even through the mask. *Walls*, he told himself. This wasn't a force field. These were the basement walls. He was getting really tired. It was hard moving through water. Much harder than moving through the air. And this water was really thick and seemed almost to be giving off some kind of gas that made him a little nauseated.

Now the voice was calling him toward the stairs. He didn't know why he was trying to make things more difficult for himself. The answer was so obvious. If he went up the stairs, they wouldn't be the same stairs he came down.

This made him a little nervous.

Where would he end up?

He was sure it wouldn't be the same trashed house he'd entered.

The woman kept calling him Tony but he knew this couldn't be *the* Tony's house. Tony was much too glamorous for a house like this. His house was probably immaculate. Marble floors. An ashtray in every room. Tony—his dad's Tony—probably had a whole collection of meat photos. He didn't want to admit it, but he could understand why his dad was obsessed with the boy.

By the time he made it to the bottom of the stairs, he felt ready to pass out. He clutched the banister and, though it took more effort than he would have liked, he lifted his head up to the steep climb ahead of him. No, this definitely wasn't the staircase he'd come down. There had to be at least twice as many stairs as he'd descended. But maybe it just seemed that way because it was always easier to go down the stairs than up.

A man stood at the top of the stairs. The man wore a meat photo as a mask just as Chad did.

If his vocabulary were bigger, he would have thought, *Kindred spirit*.

Instead, Chad held out his arms and said, "Friend."

The man turned and lifted something from behind him before tossing it down the stairs. At first Chad thought it was a bag of trash but then he realized it was the woman who'd kept calling him Tony. He thought he should move out of the way but he'd moved all he could for a while.

The woman landed on him and they both went under the water with a splash.

The large woman was very heavy and Chad had thoroughly exhausted himself and figured he would probably just die. He didn't mind. It wasn't like anyone would miss him. Ten kids from his class had already died this year and no one cared. It wasn't like he thought he'd ever make it out of middle school.

Shortly before drawing what was probably his last breath, he felt someone removing the now heavily soiled mask from his face. He had a moment where he thought that someone was going to help him up but that time never came. The person at the top of the stairs had only wanted his mask. Chad understood.

*Gotta collect 'em all*, he thought before opening his mouth and drawing in the sewer water with his final breath.

# 24

"**W**HERE ARE WE GOING?" TONY said. Now he wasn't smoking just one cigarette. He had four cigarettes shoved into the soft tissue of his meat photo mouth and was smoking all of them at the same time. It was almost like his face was becoming the meat photo.

"I'm going to the Dollar General," Kyle said.

"I thought you were going to take me back to my house so we could put the wheels on."

"Are the carts still back there?" Kyle didn't need to ask. He knew they were. He'd been watching the sparks in the rearview mirror since attaching the carts.

"Yeah," Tony said without looking.

"Then we'll get to it. Don't start pulling that Chad shit."

"Why are we going to the DG?"

"Because I want to. I need a few things. My wife doesn't go to the store anymore and my son is practically retarded. Let me have this."

"Whatever, dude."

Kyle pulled into the empty parking lot of the Dollar General.

"One year," Tony said, "my mom went to a Dollar Tree after she got her tax return and she bought one of everything. I never seen her that happy."

"Buying stuff is pretty great. Makes you feel powerful."

"She never liked Dollar General though 'cause she said it was a lie and most things in there weren't a dollar. Said it was a real rip-off."

"Your mom needs some class. The Dollar General is for finer things."

"I get it. I steal things from it all the time. I should steal some more spray paint."

Kyle stopped the car and they got out. Tony didn't bother tossing the cigarettes he was smoking. They'd burned out in the mass of meat on his face. Kyle didn't think they minded smoking in the Dollar General anyway.

A red glow came from the front door. He'd never seen that before but he also couldn't recall ever being here at this hour. Now he was more excited than ever. He tugged eagerly on the door.

"Locked," he said.

"Yeah, I don't think they're open all night."

"I need to get in there."

"Stand back," Tony said.

Kyle thought he was going to grab a rock or something but the boy, so brave, took a few steps back and charged for the front door. It shattered and Tony went spilling onto the floor on the other side. No alarms went off.

Kyle stepped through the door, his feet crunching on the broken glass. Tony lay on the floor in the middle of it, his mostly nude body now covered in cuts and oozing blood onto the floor. He stood up, his underwear already soaked in blood.

"I'll get some hydrogen peroxide and Band-Aids," Kyle said, but after looking around at the interior of the Dollar General, he knew he wouldn't be able to find those things.

Cloaked in the red light, his eyes grew wide as he surveyed the transformed interior.

Everything had been cleared from the middle of the store. Plastered on all of the walls were photos of artfully arranged meat. The Dollar General had been converted into the most beautiful art gallery Kyle had ever seen.

"Wow," Tony said in awe.

"Wow is right," Kyle said, reaching up to stroke his mask. He had a momentary urge to go back outside and fuck the meat in the trunk but he wanted to look at what was around him. Already he was thinking about stealing as many of these photos as possible.

A door toward the back of the store opened and a man wearing a black suit and a meat photo mask began walking toward them.

"My name's Neal. Can I help you?" the man said.

Kyle didn't say anything. He wondered if he and Tony had it in them to beat this man to death.

# 25

**D**ONNA RICH LOOKED AT ALL the Munch she'd set out with a rapidly increasing sense of disappointment. The best thing about living in her building was the access to the roof. She remembered moving here and posting a selfie with the caption, "Rooftop parties!" It had taken a few months for her to finally organize one and now she had ... and no one had come. She'd invited everyone from work and all of her brother's friends. It should have been around fifty people and she had purchased enough beverages and Munch for at least that many. She'd set up her speakers and had some music playing. She had curated the playlist carefully to make sure there wasn't anything on it that would offend anybody. Not just with the lyrics but with the artists' lifestyles either. It was getting harder and harder to find people with a clean record. If she had all the money in the world, she'd start a record label where all of the artists were thoroughly vetted so people wouldn't have to think so hard about it.

Now, sitting alone on the rooftop, the music still seemed sad even though she knew the band was guilty of absolutely nothing.

It was one of her favorite songs too, "Buying Things." She tried to hum along to it but wasn't feeling it. It was a perfect night. The breeze caressed her skin as she crossed over to the table to start on her second bag of Munch. She might as well eat it all if no one was coming.

She had thrown this party for a very specific reason. She had cancer. This was going to be her big reveal. Now she wondered if she would even bother telling anyone about it. She looked up at the glittering banner she'd strung across the railing. "MY DAYS ARE NUMBERED!!!" it proudly proclaimed. Now she guessed she would just have it incinerated or be buried with it when her time came.

She'd drunk so much soda she really had to pee. She was too lazy to go back to her apartment and use the restroom. Besides, what if someone showed up while she was indisposed. She'd never be able to live with herself then.

She went over to the railing, hiked up her dress and slid down her underwear, launching a powerful stream of urine over the edge.

The door to the rooftop opened and she momentarily panicked.

Dear god, what would someone think if they came to her party and found her pissing over the edge of the roof like a common street person? They might think it was a very different kind of party. But Donna wasn't that kind of person. She wasn't a sick pervert. She was just sick. Cancer.

She hoped it was Kyle from the office. She thought he was easily the cutest, most stylish guy there. She loved his lush nose hair he had growing out of one nostril. She'd never seen anything like it before. But she didn't want him to see her like this. But she couldn't stop.

Even worse, she now felt like she had to shit too.

The person stepped out of the doorway and noticed her just as she began straining to move her bowels.

She didn't recognize the person coming toward her. She was pretty sure it was a he, since he only wore a pair of underwear and didn't have any breasts. Also, it looked like he had a photo of artfully arranged meat plastered over his face. She'd been seeing this more and more lately but, like a lot of things, she didn't understand it. She figured it would probably just be some short-lived internet trend.

Her bowels emptied with a liquid rush—probably from eating too much Munch—and she felt a lot better.

The man continued to approach her and she thought about telling him he hadn't been invited but, hey, at least *someone* had shown up.

Beggars couldn't be choosers.

She stood up and realized she didn't have anything to wipe with.

"I'm sorry you had to see that," she said. But, she wondered, could this man really *see* anything? It made her feel a little better to think he couldn't. Although, if he'd just witnessed her pissing and shitting over the edge of the rooftop and still wanted anything to do with her, he might be kind of into her.

She pulled up her underwear and could feel the shit slicking her ass cheeks. "Are you here for the party? I don't recognize you with your mask on." Donna did her best to make flirtatious gestures and studied the guy as he approached her, looking for any mannerism that would tell her who the partygoer was. "Are you one of my brother's friends?"

The man didn't answer and eventually stopped in front of her. She stared at the photo of meat the person was wearing as a mask and forgot she was trying to seduce the stranger. There was something alluring about the glistening meat that pulled her into a trance.

"Meat photo," the man whispered.

Donna was finding it hard to concentrate. "Huh?"

"Meat photo," the man said forcefully.

"Meat photo," she repeated. "Wha—"

The man's arms shot up and shoved Donna hard in the chest and she was launched over the edge of the rooftop. As she fell, Donna wasn't sure if she was screaming because her death was happening a lot quicker than she'd expected, or if she was upset that she would never see that beautiful photo of meat again. Maybe she'd been looking forward to dying from cancer. All she knew for sure was that she was glad it would be quick.

# 26

**A**GNES WAS TIRED AND HUNGRY. She regretted not bringing more Munch with her. She'd brought as much as she could carry but that didn't last her more than five blocks. Maybe she could stop at the gas station and get some more. No. Something told her she had to keep going. She had to find the man without a face with the huge meat photo.

It was dark in the city. Only about half the street lights worked where she lived. She could get to the faceless man a lot quicker if she had a car. But Kyle had taken their car to hang out with Tony again. And who knew when he'd be back home. Usually when he hung out with Tony he wouldn't be back until the sun came up. And Agnes couldn't wait for that. She had to get to the meat photo in her dreams.

It felt like Agnes had been walking for hours but she hadn't even made it to the main road. Her feet and legs felt swollen and she couldn't remember the last time she'd stood upright for this long. She couldn't remember the last time she walked this far.

She was out of breath when she made it to the main road. The traffic was sparse this late at night. She spotted something moving down the street, coming closer to her. Agnes was confused by the shape of it. It was much smaller than a car but moved at a decent speed. She squinted at it once it rolled under a streetlamp. It was a person in a motorized chair, driving along on the road like it was a car. The person appeared to have a condition that left their limbs in atrophy and it looked as though they had something on their face. The person zoomed past her, going in the opposite direction.

She took a few breaths and headed toward the harsh fluorescent lights of the gas station. By the time she made it to the parking lot she had to stop again to catch her breath. Her clothes were soaked in sweat and she knew she needed more Munch to feel better.

There were no cars at the pumps and it didn't appear that anyone other than the clerk was inside. She pushed open the door and was immediately greeted with a display of Munch. She grabbed a bag, ripped it open, and began devouring it.

"Ya gotta pay first!" the clerk yelled.

She stared at the clerk. He was a skinny man that looked like he lived off of cigarettes and coffee. His face was worn and leathery and he was missing half his teeth. Agnes thought he might not be so moody if he ate some Munch.

"I have a condition," she said. "I gotta have my Munch or I'm gonna pass out."

"I don't give a good god damn if you're gonna die, lady. Ya gotta pay for the Munch 'for ya eat it!"

She took her time gathering up all the Munch she could, popping some of the bags open accidently when she gripped them too tight.

The clerk berated her. "I'm sick 'n' tired of ya junkies comin' in here and eating all the Munch. I cain't keep the shelves stocked. An' then ya'll ransack the place like a bunch of wild boars."

Agnes approached the counter, piled all the bags on it, and finished off the bag of Munch she'd started. She dropped the empty bag on the counter while the clerk glared at her and continued to ring up her purchase.

She noticed a display of large postcards beside the register. Each one was a photo of meat. She grabbed a handful of them with her Munch-covered hands. They were all so beautiful and she felt she needed to buy all of them. But something told her she only needed one. She flipped through them until her heart nearly stopped. She was certain the one she was looking at was the one from her dream.

"I need this." She showed the postcard to the clerk.

"Don't know why everyone wants those damn things. Ugly as sin if ya ask me."

"Well, I didn't."

"Didn't what?"

"Ask you."

The clerk huffed and punched something on the register keys, bagged up her bags of Munch, and gave her the total. She pulled the cash out of her bra and tried to hand it to him.

"Aw naw," the clerk said. "Ain't takin' your sweaty titty money."

"Ain't nothing wrong with it." She shoved it in his direction.

The clerk made a bug-eyed expression. "I don't give a fuck if it's a million dollars. Would ya take money from me if I pulled it out of my arsehole? You nasty. Ya smell like rotten meat."

She threw the cash on the counter and grabbed the bags of Munch and her postcard of meat.

"Nah!" The clerk tried to grab the bags from her.

Bags of Munch popped and exploded into the air. The two wrestled over the Munch.

"My money's good!" she shouted.

"No titty money!"

Agnes wrenched the bags from the clerk and ran out the door. She ran around the building and across the empty parking lot of an abandoned K-mart, heading toward a cluster of trees. She could hear the clerk shouting but couldn't understand what he was saying. Her heart was pounding and she thought she might faint before she made it to safety. Once she made it to the group of trees, she collapsed, took a few minutes to catch her breath, and opened a bag of Munch. She needed to eat. She needed to restore her energy.

The dim light from the parking lot was enough for her to see what she was looking for. She dug around in the bags until she found her postcard. She ran her hand over the glossy photo and imagined she was stroking the photo from her dreams. It made her wet and she thought about her meat man at home. She knew she could bring her meat man to life if she could find the faceless man. She was thinking of him like he was the great and powerful Oz who could give her everything she wanted.

Agnes lifted the postcard to her face. She didn't know how to make it stay on. Something told her she needed to wear it. It was the only way the faceless man would let her in when she arrived. She looked at the bags of Munch around her and picked up an empty one and slipped it on her head like a hat. She slid the postcard under the edge of the bag to hold it in place and knew she was ready to meet the faceless man and finally have the meat photo of her dreams.

# 27

"**FEEL FREE TO LOOK AROUND,**" Neal said, gesturing around the Dollar General, which looked huge now that the aisles filled with low-priced garbage had been removed.

Kyle knew he had come here to pick up a couple of things but he couldn't remember what those items were. This was . . . so much better. He'd never seen this many photos of artfully arranged meat in one place.

Tony lit a couple of cigarettes and stuck them in his meat hole amidst the previously burned-out ones.

Kyle was pretty sure Neal looked alarmed when he did this. Kyle stroked his own meat photo, wondering when his would finally fuse with his face and turn him into the perfect man. Probably never. That's why he liked Tony so much. For a kid his age, he was really advanced.

"C'mon," Kyle said. "Let's go look." He began walking to one of the back corners, shrouded in that eerie red light. Tony followed him.

They began studying one of the meat photos on the wall. It wasn't artfully framed or anything like that. Just stuck up to the wall with some sort of adhesive or maybe even tape. At least the guy hadn't stapled it. That seemed sacrilegious.

"What do you think?" Kyle said.

"I think this place is pretty fucking awesome," Tony said. "Little sad they don't sell cigarettes though."

"You could ask. Maybe he moved them to the back or something."

"Nah. I got plenty. I keep a couple packs shoved up my ass so my mom doesn't find 'em and smoke 'em."

"Be careful with that."

"It's real roomy back there."

"Nature's pocket."

Together, they drifted down the wall, looking at all the photos of meat. They were all slightly different—different cuts of meat from different angles and under different lighting—but, still, there was a similarity to each of them.

"You take all these pictures?" Kyle called to Neal.

"Yes. It's my life's work."

"Fuckin' legend," Tony muttered under his breath.

"They're all very nice."

"I don't really need your approval," Neal said.

"Okay, buddy," Kyle returned.

The way Tony was lost in all the photos sent a spike of jealousy through Kyle. He knew that if Neal were to approach Tony and suggest that he could become his apprentice if they slaughtered Kyle and stuffed him into a dumpster in the back, Tony would unhesitatingly say yes.

"This guy's kind of a dick," Kyle said to Tony. He knew he had to turn Tony against Neal as quickly as possible or risk losing him. He really wanted to replace Chad with Tony and couldn't bear the thought of going home and looking at Chad's dumb fucking face again.

Tony offered nothing in return and Kyle knew he was in trouble.

"You selling them?" Kyle thought if he could buy one and give it to Tony, that might keep him in the boy's good graces.

"Nope. They're just to look at. Do you know how much these things are going to be worth in a few years?"

"Probably a pretty penny."

Neal forced out a harsh laugh and said, "That's an understatement. This is my retirement."

Kyle's retirement plan was to kill Agnes and hope her life insurance policy paid off. He wasn't sure, but he might get rid of Chad too, since the boy was mostly worthless. He briefly entertained the thought of he and Tony staying at some fancy tropical island, drinking expensive drinks and splashing around in the ocean.

"You know," Kyle spoke lowly to Tony, "these could all be ours."

"I want them," Tony said. "I need all of them."

Kyle tried to formulate a plan as they continued looking at the meat photos. He was pretty sure they were going to have to kill Neal.

"Have you ever killed anyone before?" Kyle asked Tony.

"My younger sister. But that was years ago."

"How did you feel about it?"

Tony shrugged. "Okay, I guess. I never got caught, so that was pretty cool. Made Mom happy. One less mouth to feed."

Kyle had once struck an elderly man on a bicycle with his car. He had driven away before checking on the guy and had avoided watching the news for at least a month afterward, so he couldn't really say for sure if he'd killed anyone or not. Now he wished he had known the outcome. He thought it would be a lot easier if he already had one murder under his belt.

Before they could turn the next corner to begin looking at the photos on that wall, Neal was right behind them.

"Whoa, man," Kyle said. "How 'bout giving us a little space?"

"I'm sorry, but I have to ask about that mask."

Kyle, naturally assuming he was referring to him, said, "What? I pulled it off some guy outside a nursing home."

"Not yours. His." Neal was already reaching his hand out to stroke Tony's face. Before he got there, he stopped. "I'm sorry. Is it okay?"

"I don't fuckin' care," Tony said.

Kyle watched jealously as Neal stroked the meat on Tony's face, because now, it really didn't seem like a photo of meat at all. It looked like actual meat, as though the photo had come to life and was parasitically clinging to Tony's face.

"How long have you had this?"

"I don't know. Probably had it forever. Just put it on tonight."

"I think it might be an original."

Kyle butted in. "An original Don Tross?"

Neal cast a withering glare at him. "Do you think Don Tross was the first person to do this? No. He's a fucking TV hack. These have been around since . . . well, pretty much since photography was invented."

"That's pretty cool, I guess," Kyle said. "How much you think we can get for it?"

Neal cocked his head, continuing to stroke the meat. "Not sure. Something like this is practically priceless. You could get whatever somebody is willing to pay for it."

Kyle thought about decapitating Tony.

Neal stroked the mask, squeezed it like it was a breast or something, becoming visibly excited.

"Easy now," Kyle said.

Embarrassed, Neal retracted his hand. "I'm so sorry. I'll leave you two alone. It's just . . . it's just so beautiful."

As Neal wandered back into the red light, Kyle was pretty sure he was crying.

Tony and Kyle continued looking at the photos while Kyle formulated some ideas.

Kyle put his hands on Tony's shoulders and said, "You stay here, little buddy. I'm going to go have a word with Neal."

"You gonna kill him?"

"Is that what you want?"

"Might be kind of fun."

"We'll see."

"*We'll see*," Tony mocked him like Kyle was his parent or something.

When Kyle approached Neal, Neal was looking at his phone, scrolling through photos of meat. Kyle was pretty sure he saw a tear splash onto the screen's surface.

"You really like the boy's meat photo, huh?" Kyle said.

"I've never seen anything so beautiful."

"How much would you be willing to give for it?"

"Oh, I'm an artist. I could never afford something like that. Not right now anyway."

"But . . . would you trade it for all the photos you have on the walls?"

Neal didn't even have to think about it. "Well, sure, but I don't think that would be a fair trade."

"I'd consider it an investment. I think you're going to be huge."

"Are we . . . do we have a deal?"

Kyle didn't have to think twice. He thought about driving around with all those meat photos in his car. He'd be the coolest guy in town, if he wasn't already.

"Tony!" Kyle called. "Come 'ere!" He knew the kid didn't like to be bossed around but he came right over.

"What's up?" Tony said.

"We're trading your mask for all the photos in here. That okay?"

"I don't care. As long as I can get another one. Kind of bored with this one anyway."

"Awesome," Kyle said.

"I've never had anything this good happen to me," Neal said. He eagerly reached down to remove the mask from Tony's face. It didn't want to come off. "Just as I thought. It's fused to his face."

"What's that mean?" Tony said.

"It means it's not going to come off," Kyle said.

"Maybe . . . surgery," Tony said.

"That would ruin everything," Neal said. "It would damage it. Do you know how many people this has probably absorbed over the years?"

"I don't know. A lot?" Kyle said.

"That's right," Neal said. "A whole fucking lot."

"I don't mind leaving the boy too," Kyle said. Sure, he would feel bad about it until he went to bed that morning, but how many boys had there been in the past. True, Tony seemed perfect for now, but Aaron had seemed perfect last summer, and Devon had seemed perfect the winter prior. Kyle felt pretty sure he'd be okay with his decision. Who knew? Maybe Chad would even come around and figure out how to be a cool guy and not some lazy slug.

Neal placed his hands on Tony's shoulders. "How do you feel about that, big guy?"

"As long as you can keep me in cigarettes, I don't mind."

"I think I can do that."

"Great!" Kyle said. He was already getting bored. "I'll just collect my payment and be on my way."

"It's been a pleasure doing business with you," Neal said.

"This guy's my best friend now," Tony said, and Kyle thought he could hear the bile in his voice. Kyle knew Tony would be sorry.

# 28

**B**ECKY AND KAREN WERE TWINS. They were only fifteen and had no idea why their parents had named them Becky and Karen. But none of that mattered now. What mattered was that they were in a car filled with meat and cruising to a party in the nice part of town.

Karen was scrolling through her phone, looking at pictures of the party they were going to.

Becky was driving, poorly, mostly on the sidewalk and the opposite side of the road.

"Did you see what Justin was wearing?" Karen said. "He wears one on the front *and* the back of his head."

"He's so cool. He almost fingered me at camp but he had poison oak all over his hands."

"That's so hot."

"They're going to flip out when they see what we got."

"What do we got?!" Karen called.

"A carful of meat!"

"What do we got?!"

"A carful of meat!"

"Fuck *yeah!*"

Karen turned the radio up. The song, "Beautiful Piles of Meat," was the song of the summer. It was so catchy and danceable that both of the girls began singing along to it.

"Pull some of that meat up here," Becky said.

Karen twisted around in her seat and began dragging up handfuls of meat.

"Put some right in my lap," Becky said.

Karen obeyed, putting a cut of meat between Becky's legs, the blood smearing all over her ivory thighs.

"Fuck yeah," Becky said. "Will you rub some on my face?"

Karen laughed. "Not until I stuff my bra with some."

She shoved some meat in her bra and then grabbed a cut and began rubbing it on Becky's face, all while dancing and singing to the music. Becky, too, was dancing along and driving even more recklessly.

"We should put our masks on before we get there," Becky said.

"Should have put 'em on before we even left the house."

Karen reached into the glove compartment and pulled out the two meat photo masks the girls had bought at the mall earlier. She fixed Becky's on first. This did not help her driving at all. Then she put on her own mask and felt immediately cooler and more stylish.

"Whoa!" Becky said. "I didn't think I'd be able to see out of it but . . . I think everything looks better?"

"Totally," Karen said.

Karen reached into the back seat to grab some more meat. When they got to the party, she wanted them to roll up in the car, open the doors, and have all that delicious meat slide out around them. They'd instantly be the most popular kids in class after that.

But she didn't grab meat. Or, it *was* meat, technically, but it was still attached to someone.

The figure sat up in the back seat.

"Jeremy?" Karen said.

"What the fuck, Kare," Becky said.

"Meat photo," the guy in the back said.

"Totally," Karen said.

"Right on," Becky said.

"Meat photo," the guy said.

"Fuck yeah," Karen said. "Meat photo. Isn't mine bad ass?"

"Totally," Becky said.

"Meat photo," the guy repeated.

Karen was looking forward to being the most popular girl at the party and was starting to find the new guy annoying. She really needed to focus on their arrival and how the meat was going to spill out of the car when they opened the doors. "Uh, yeah, duh. We all have meat photo masks. You don't have to keep saying that. Besides, ours are new and yours looks a little ragged." She rubbed the meat in her bra and moaned. "So new and hot."

Becky said, "Yeah, meat photo."

The guy said, "Meat photo," before lunging into the front seat and grabbing the steering wheel and jerking it toward the center line.

"Oh my god!" Becky screamed. "What are you doing?! Let go!"

Karen slapped at the guy. "Stop it! Stop it!" She grabbed at his mask to pull it off but it was fused to his face.

The sound of a semi's horn caught both of the girls' attention. Karen's thoughts were filled with disappointment because she knew they weren't going to make it to the party and Becky's only thought was, "Oh my god! The accident is going to fuck up my face!" right before they plowed head first into the oncoming semi and the car exploded into a ball of fire.

# 29

THE GREAT MIGRATION. THAT'S WHAT his parents had called it. It happened every thousand years, they'd told him. Everyone would flock to one spot, compelled to be there by some unknown force. But he knew what the force was. His parents had named him after it. They had told him he was the chosen one. They told him the Great Migration would happen one day and he would hold the source of its power. They'd told him the world would be reborn then and he would rule everything. It was something they'd read in a fortune cookie so it had to be true.

Ancient Evil had always hated his name as a kid. His parents had told him it was a necessity. All of his classmates had made fun of him. Told him he was too plain to be named Ancient Evil. That no one would remember him and no one could remember his face because he looked so generic. They called him Plain Jane and Forgettable Dave instead of his real name.

But once he grew up, he showed them. He'd gone to college, the first in his family, and picked up a job working in a gallery in the evening. He was the host and sold the artwork to anyone who could afford it. The gallery only exhibited photos of meat. Seeing meat day in and day out had desensitized him to the point that he no longer looked at meat. He loathed meat. Got to the point where he couldn't stand the sight of it, the smell of it, the taste of it. It made him gag and he became a vegetarian.

Then one day a large photo of meat arrived to be displayed. It was framed in ornate gold and appeared to be very old. But looks could be deceiving. The photo consisted of piles of glistening meat on a cutting board, a knife, an overturned goblet with meat running from it, and an extinguished candle with wisps of smoke. It was mesmerizing. Ancient Evil couldn't be sure if it was a photo or painting. It looked like a painting but, after studying it, he was certain it was a photo. The photo's title was "Meat Photo" and the artist was Neal Little. It was amazing and life changing and he couldn't get enough of it.

And then his boss found out he was vegetarian. He told him he couldn't have a vegetarian selling the meat art. So that night, his final night at the gallery, he stole "Meat Photo," along with a smaller print of the photo, and waited for the Great Migration and what it would bring.

# 30

JACOB OWNED A MEAT MARKET HE named Jacob's
Meat. He never thought in a million years it would be the most
popular meat market in the city. Ever since the sun had set the
place had been packed. It reminded him of those Black Friday sales
you see on TV. People were fighting over his meat, pushing and shoving one another to get whatever they could get their hands on. He
would've closed the store hours ago, at 9 PM like he did every day,
but the crowd was so thick and dangerous he didn't dare walk out
from behind the counter. Besides, he was selling more meat in one
day than he usually did in a year. How could he tell these people no?

At one point he'd run out of meat and he wasn't sure what he was
going to do. The people looked desperate. And then he watched as
an elderly woman wearing a photo of meat as a mask beat a young
boy to death because he had grabbed the last package of bacon.

That's when inspiration hit. He'd screamed at the people close to
the dead child to hand him the body. Two men had hoisted the child
over the counter and Jacob had gotten to work. He worked as quickly
as he could to butcher the boy, weighed each portion, and packaged
the meat. As quickly as he'd placed the meat on the counter it was
snatched up. Another dead body was flung over the counter at him

and he hadn't stopped since.

The people in the store were rabid for the meat. He realized he could put any price on the meat and the people would pay it. After a few hours he noticed the clients had changed. Everyone entering the store now was naked but wore a photo of meat as a mask like the old woman who'd beat the first boy to death. He wasn't sure what this meant but he didn't have time to ask or think about it.

He was exhausted and sweaty and covered in blood and the crowd never stopped. Jacob wasn't sure what to do. How was he going to shut down the market and clean up? A delivery truck would arrive in the morning to deliver another load of meat but it wouldn't be enough.

He really only had two options:

1. He could start a small fire. He was hesitant to burn the entire place to the ground because it was his life's work and the thought of starting another butchery was exhausting and overwhelming. Plus, it was probably a crime. Insurance fraud or something. He didn't think the fire department would understand if he told them he had to start a small fire to get people to leave. Would the people even leave? He wasn't sure they would.

2. He could join them and put on a meat photo mask. He didn't know where everyone was getting theirs but thought he could perhaps trade some meat for one of their masks. The problem with this was that Jacob was a contrarian. He wasn't a joiner. He didn't really have an opinion one way or the other about the masks but would refuse to wear one just because everyone else was doing it and was philosophically minded enough that he could come up with a thousand reasons why they were dumb.

When the first person smashed one of the display cases with a fire extinguisher and began shoving handfuls of meat down his pants, Jacob's mind was made up. He hadn't realized the display case on the side wall still had some meat in it. The crowd was so thick it was hard to see anything. How dare they steal from him. He should have been like some kind of priest or holy man to these people and this was how they treated him. Now others were standing at the busted case helping themselves as he feverishly worked to ring people up.

An enormous crash came from somewhere outside and Jacob felt the building shake. He had no idea what had caused it and there was no time to check.

"One moment please," he said to the palsied old woman on the other side of the register.

He quickly walked through the swinging doors behind the counter, hearing the shouts of dismay and cries of anger coming from the floor. He was a little out of his head. He threw open the doors to the smoker and, using a shovel that was normally for scooping out the ashes, he began dragging the burning wood out of the smoker and onto the floor. He grabbed some butcher paper and unfurled it over the flames. That should do it. And sure, it looked a little like arson, but he was certain he could talk his way out of it and get the necessary insurance money to make repairs.

The fire spread much more quickly than he would have thought.

He walked back out to the register, plumes of smoke behind him. He thought this would worry or panic people and many of them would leave.

The fire alarm started up, deafening, so loud it felt like the world was vibrating around him and his brain was being turned into jelly.

He picked up the mouthpiece to the store intercom and said, "Everyone needs to vacate the store immediately!"

No one vacated the store immediately except him. He quickly stuffed the money from the register in his pockets and ran out the front door. He stood outside and watched the people through the large window at the front of the store, listening for sirens in the distance. He heard nothing. A few people came out carrying armloads of meat but the others were still running around in the store, even as the flames spread. Soon, most of the people who came out were on fire. They'd burst through the front door, completely ablaze, their arms loaded with meat and go running into the night. He wished he'd captured some of this on his phone but that was what everyone else was doing and he'd always told people he had a brain, therefore a memory, and didn't need to record shit because everything didn't have to be performative. Plus, there was the insurance fraud thing again and he didn't want to do anything that could incriminate him.

A large man who was mostly on fire shambled to him from outside the store. Jacob squinted his eyes beyond the man and noticed a large fire out on one of the main drags. Could this man be a survivor from the awful crash he'd heard only moments before but was too distracted by his rabid customers to investigate?

Clearly, this guy had not come from the store and had caught fire somewhere else.

"Can I help you?" Jacob said, even though he didn't really care.

"Meat photo," the man said.

"Yeah, whatever, fuck your meat photo, dude. You know what?

I'd like to fuck your meat photo with your dead dad's dick. I know your dad's dead because if I'd had a son like you, I would have killed myself before your fucking slut mom could bring you home from the baby farm."

"Meat photo."

"Good comeback. Why don't you do something else edgy like go listen to Marilyn Manson or watch a Quentin Tarantino film, you fucking normie piece of shit. Oh, what are you going to say next? 'Let people like things'? Fuck off."

"Meat photo."

But Jacob couldn't come back with anything else because the man's sizeable hand had punched through his neck and now had his esophagus clenched in his fist. Also, because the man was still on fire, Jacob was now on fire too. The last thing Jacob saw was his life's work burning to the ground in the reflection of the man's glossy meat photo mask.

# 31

**K**YLE CONTINUED TO DRIVE AROUND the suburbs surrounding the Dollar General. There was a feverish excitement in the air as he cruised through the streets with his windows down, already missing the smell of Tony's cigarette smoke. Maybe he'd stop at a gas station and pick up a pack. He used to love smoking. He'd had to stop when Chad was born because, well, because Agnes had made him stop doing anything fun. He'd even had to burn most of his USB drives.

"They'll take Chad if they ever find them!" she had cried out.

What a fucking cunt. And now that she was terminally ill and he'd lost Tony, he thought he could really put what was on those USB drives to work. Sure, maybe Chad would still be around, but Kyle was planning on either having him committed or framing him or just making him live outside the second Agnes was out of the picture.

"This guy's my best friend now." Tony's cold and callus final words to Kyle were still rattling around in his head when he saw an old woman wandering the side of the road, nude, a giant gray bush between her legs and a meat photo on her face. No, it wasn't a meat photo. It was a bag of Munch. No, it was a bag of Munch holding a meat photo over her face. Too fucking poor to even score something to hold the photo in place like a proper mask. Must be a homeless person or something.

He'd never had a problem getting a handjob or blowjob from a homeless person and, after an evening spent with Tony and surrounded by so many meat photos, he could use some relief.

He pulled the car up alongside the woman.

"Hey, baby!" he called.

She approached the car.

Fuck. As she got closer, he realized it was Agnes. Total boner killer. He jammed his foot down on the accelerator and peeled away.

# 32

**D**ENNIS HAD NEVER BEEN this far up inside Bret before.

"Jesus," Dennis said. "I'm almost up to my elbow."

Bret turned and looked over his shoulder. Dennis was sure he wore a totally beatific, blissed-out expression but he couldn't be sure because of the meat photo mask. Only . . . he kind of could. Was it possible for these eyeless, mouthless masks to convey expressions?

Hell, he'd answered his own question. If he was in Bret's rectum all the way up to his elbow, anything was possible.

Normally, Dennis and Bret retired to one of their bedrooms to do this kind of thing but they'd been watching MeatTV and drinking a lot and their judgment had eroded and they were unable to contain themselves.

Dennis reached around and felt for Bret's tumescent cock. He was harder than he'd ever been. He rubbed the pearl of glistening precum gathered on the tip of Bret's cock.

Dennis began working his fist in and out of Bret.

"We're gonna paint this whole place white," he drunkenly slurred.

"White with come!" Bret shouted. He always had trouble controlling the volume of his own voice when he'd been drinking.

"There's gonna be so much come. Want me to go a little further?"

"I want you to put the other fist in."

Dennis didn't know about this. He thought they'd probably both regret it tomorrow, but he was also curious. Could he do it? Could Bret take it?

"Put it in!" Bret said viciously.

Then, what Dennis was afraid of happened. He heard a bedroom door creak open behind him. They'd woken Chuck up. Chuck was always such a buzzkill.

"What the hell are you guys doing?"

Whatever. Dennis didn't care. He held up his free hand and said, "Going in with two hands!" Okay, maybe he was a little drunker than he thought.

Chuck wore a meat photo mask because he slept in it. He said the other side was coated in various beauty products that kept him from aging but Dennis was pretty sure he just liked sleeping in the mask. It was like a security blanket or something.

"You weren't going to invite me?" Chuck said.

Dennis was surprised by this. While both he and Bret had hooked up with Chuck here and there, Chuck never wanted to take part in their antics. It had been a dream of Dennis's that they could all get along enough to do something like this but, despite all of his scheming and plotting, he'd never been able to engineer it. Tonight, however, it looked like fortune was going to shine on him.

Dennis thrust his buttocks toward Chuck and said, "Lube that fist up and dive right in, I'm stretched to the max."

Chuck slid his bikini briefs down his legs, snatched up the bottle of lube and . . . began lubing up his head.

Dennis had a moment where he wondered if an adult male head could fit in his asshole but cast his doubts aside. It was about the adventure.

"I like the way you think, Chuck," Dennis said.

"You're about to get an assful of meat," Chuck said.

"Make it hurt, buddy. Make it hurt."

Once slicked with enough lube, Chuck got down on his knees and began working the crown of his head into Dennis's gaping and prolapsed rectum. Dennis began sliding his free hand into Bret.

"We're gonna be like the human centipede of fisting!" Bret shouted.

"No way, man," Dennis said. "Chuck's using his head."

"He's putting his head in your ass?!"

"You bet."

"Wild!"

Dennis felt Chuck's head break the seal and it was pretty smooth sailing until he reached the widest part of his head. Dennis thought his hip bones were going to break apart but he loved the sensation. He imagined, from here on out, cruising for people with the largest heads. But they couldn't be like fat heads. He wanted them to be large and firm. Someone with a fat head would be like getting fucked with a semi-erect cock, which would make him sad and self-conscious.

Dennis heard another door open and was momentarily alarmed. He was pretty sure no one else lived in the apartment. Then Chuck forced his head the rest of the way in and he felt the glorious pressure in his bowels. It was enough to distract him from the intruder.

When he came back to reality, there was a man, also in a meat photo mask, standing right beside him.

"Meat photo," the man said.

"Yeah, man, we all have them. Hop on, if that's what you're here for. We might break some kind of record tonight. At least of personal bests."

"Meat photo," the man repeated.

"How 'bout you put that meat photo in Chuck's ass," Dennis said.

But the man in the mask reached out and deftly shucked the skin from Dennis's head, leaving nothing but the meat photo. The man in the mask spent the next several minutes forcing the entirety of Dennis into Bret. Then the entirety of Chuck into Bret.

"I don't feel very comfortable right now!" Bret shouted.

"Meat photo," the guy said.

He stood behind Bret and backed up. The man got a running start and dived straight into Bret's asshole. For a brief second, Bret thought he was the Turducken of fisting before he exploded and painted the living room in his, Dennis's, and Chuck's innards.

The man lay in the middle of the living room floor, among the remains of the other three men, and said, "Meat photo."

# 33

**A**GNES STUMBLED OUT OF THE wooded area nude, her thoughts no longer hers. The meat photo was now something bigger than her. Something bigger than the world. The meat photo was guiding her to something that beckoned her.

A car had stopped and the person said something she could no longer understand. Language meant nothing now. The person had sped off into the night.

If Agnes could feel pain she would be screaming in agony as the meat photo adhered to her face, becoming one with it, feeding off her.

She started off down the road, ignorant of the world around her.

"Meat photo."

In the distance she saw a beam of neon red light shooting into the sky. It was glorious and she knew it was the source of energy she needed. It would feed her. It would be orgasmic. She had to have it. She began her journey toward it.

"Meat photo."

# 34

"**THANK YOU FOR COMING, FATHER** Peters."

Father Peters stepped inside the home of Stephanie Gash and took a look around at all of the religious icons hung on the wall. He redoubled his grip on his medicine bag. The house was cold and had an odd odor. It reminded him of a meat locker but as if the meat had gone bad.

"How is she?" Father Peters said.

Stephanie Gash had a short and heavily highlighted hairdo so meticulously styled to perfection that Father Peters wondered if it was a wig. Her face was worn and puffy from crying, her makeup a mess, as if she'd reapplied it without washing the old spackle off first. Her outfit looked like she'd seen a mannequin in the junior's section at a Kohl's and she'd bought the exact same outfit because she thought it would make her look trendy and hip. It didn't. It made her look desperate and sad and bloated. The outfit was a size or two too small for the middle-aged woman. Her appearance seemed fitting for the occasion.

"Not well," Stephanie said. "She's this way."

She pointed toward a hallway off the living room and made to lead Father Peters. Father Peters grabbed her shoulder to stop her. She turned to look at him.

"I'm sorry," he said. "I can't perform the rites with you in the room. This is between McKayla and god. You must understand . . ."

Stephanie took a deep breath and choked back a sob. She clutched at the top of her shirt as if looking for the loop of pearls that weren't there. She nodded and pointed down the hall again just as something unholy bellowed.

"Meat photo!"

Stephanie sobbed. "It's much worse than when we spoke!"

Father Peters nodded and proceeded down the hallway, toward the open door at the end. The smell of rotten meat was too much and he buried his nose in the crook of his elbow. Before he could make it to the bedroom door, McKayla growled.

"Meat photo."

Father Peters stopped in the open doorway and took in the scene. The room had been stripped of everything except a bed without any sheets or covers. A young girl in her underwear lay supine on the bed. Her wrists and ankles were bound and tied to the legs of the bed. Her face was a mass of swimming meat, constantly twisting and morphing. The smell of rotten meat was overpowering.

Father Peters had never seen such a thing in all his years of performing exorcisms. He was caught off guard and wasn't sure if he should proceed. He'd witnessed some meat photo possessions but he'd never seen one this bad. Maybe he should make a few phone calls. Call Father Michaels to see if he'd ever witnessed such a thing. Father Michaels had more experience than he did.

"Meat photo," McKayla said. Her voice sounded like an eighty-year-old smoker.

Father Peters dropped his arm covering his face and let the stench hit him full force. He stepped inside the room and shut the door. He approached the bed and opened his bag, pulling all the tools he would need from within it.

"Meat photo," McKayla whispered.

Father Peters began reciting the exorcism rites, splashing McKayla with the holy water. She did not react, only repeated "meat photo" periodically and pulled on her restraints. After the first round of recital Father Peters stared at the swarm of moving meat that had replaced McKayla's face. He crouched down and got on his knees so he could be closer to her.

"What are your sins, McKayla. Huh? Were you a dirty little slut? Giving handjobs to the other boys? Sucking them off? Letting them stick it in your tight little ass?" Father Peters could feel himself getting hard asking McKayla these questions but he had to know. He had to know her sins and the name of the demon within her if he were to cast them out. "Were you a thieving cunt? Steal some candy from the corner store? Maybe you diddled your daddy? Is that it? Fucked your daddy, did you?"

"Meat photo."

Father Peters had little patience. He grabbed McKayla by the shoulders and began to shake her violently. "Tell me, you fucking come bucket! You've fucked everyone else in this town and you won't even give me a handjob! You fucking cock tease! You'll go to hell for this! God will fuck you in your tight little ass and rip your cunt in two!" He let go of McKayla and let her fall back on the bed.

"Meat photo."

"What are you doing?!"

He hadn't heard Stephanie open the bedroom door. She stood in the doorway, looking mortified.

"Get me some fucking barbecue sauce!" Father Peters shouted.

Stephanie flinched and trembled but didn't move.

"Now! Now!"

She snapped out of her shock and shot out of the room.

He called after her. "Your daughter is a slut!"

"Meat photo," McKayla said.

Father Peters clenched his fist and brandished it at the girl. "I'll show you." He shook his fist at her meat face. "Fucking cunt."

Stephanie reappeared with a bottle of A1 and handed it to Father Peters.

"This isn't barbecue sauce, you fucking cow!"

"It's sauce," Stephanie Gash wept. "Isn't it close enough?"

Father Peters, exasperated, massaged his temples. "If someone asks for ketchup on their hot, plump footlong, do you put mustard on it?"

Stephanie looked confused.

"Do you?!" Father Peters barked.

The woman's mouth curved down in a violent tremble.

"No! You absolutely do not fucking use mustard instead of ketchup. Now go get me some fucking barbecue sauce. I don't care if you have to go to the store. That'll give me even more time to prepare McKayla here."

"I'll look harder," Stephanie said.

"Meat photo," McKayla growled.

"Do that," Father Peters said. "Look . . . harder."

The plump woman disappeared from the doorway.

"Seriously, what did she except me to do with this?" Father Peters twisted the cap off the A1 and took a slug. He leaned back over McKayla, hoping he would hear Stephanie Gash get into her car and pull away. He didn't.

"Meat photo," the girl growled before spitting something onto Father Peters' overcoat. It looked like a combination of old blood and congealed fat and smelled even more rotten than the room.

"Just tell me what you'd want me to do to you if your mom wasn't here."

"Meat photo," the girl growled.

"You like meat, huh, you little slut. Little cock goblin. You like old dirty meat, don't you? Like to put it on your face. You like it when it gets in your hair and eyes. I bet you let all those boys at school put their meat all over you, don't you? Bet you like it when they put their meat in you. You want to be covered with meat inside and out, you dirty little demon girl."

He placed a hand on the meat covering the girl's face.

He was surprised by Stephanie Gash in the doorway behind him.

"Father Peters!" she called.

He quickly snapped his hand back. "Little bitch tried to bite me!" he said.

"I found some barbecue sauce," Stephanie said.

"Meat photo," the girl growled.

"Give it here," Father Peters said.

The woman dropped three containers of McDonald's barbecue sauce into his hand.

"I guess this'll have to do," he said.

"It's all I have," Stephanie said.

"It's a good thing you didn't have to go to the store," Father Peters said. "You know, I've never experienced a single carnal pleasure, although it's all I think about. I'm always waiting for the thing that's going to make me finally commit that most egregious of sins."

Stephanie smirked. "It's just fucking. People do it all the time."

"They haven't taken the vow."

"That sounds made up. You're making your life unnecessarily difficult. My daughter has a demon in her. I didn't ask for it."

"You're really starting to piss me off," Father Peters said.

"Just telling it like it is."

"Okay, well, you're fat and way too old to be dressed like that.

Your house is a wreck and you allowed your daughter to become possessed by a demon and, judging from what my parishioners have said about her, that's probably the best outcome they could have predicted for her. Just telling it like it is. Do you have anything else you'd like to say to me?"

Stephanie Gash said nothing.

"Good. Then how 'bout keeping your cow mouth shut while I do what you asked me here to do."

Father Peters reached into his bag and pulled out an acetylene torch. He lit it and looked excitedly at the flame.

"Oh, god, what are you going to do?"

"I thought I told you to keep your mouth shut. If you must know, the mask has attached itself to your daughter's face. This meat photo thing is no different than heavy metal music in the 80s. Kids never know what they're messing with. It all seems so trendy and hip and fun . . . until the demons get in. Not everyone is receptive to it. A lot of people will just be idiots walking around with photos of meat on their faces. But some people, the ones most receptive to possession . . . like really dumb people and those with loose morals, will find themselves on a dark path driven by the demons they've allowed in. I see it every day. Let me, the expert, do what I need to do. You can either watch or you can get out. Although I would advise that you stay if you want your daughter to remain in a mostly unsullied state. As I stated before, I never know when my carnal desires will get the best of me."

"You're a sick man."

"I, Ms. Gash, am a sick man who makes people better."

Father Peters leaned over the bed and touched the torch to the meat on McKayla's face while Stephanie Gash pressed herself up against one of the walls and began screaming. McKayla began kicking her legs and throwing herself around while shouting, "Meat photo! Meat photo! Meat photo!"

The meat on her face charred and sizzled, rivulets of fat soaking the bed. Father Peters' stomach growled. Once the meat was nearly blackened and cooked through, Father Peters bellowed, "Prepare the sauce!"

"What?" Stephanie Gash sounded confused.

"Prepare the sauce!"

"I don't know what you mean!"

"Pull back the foil on the stupid little containers, you dumb bitch!" Father Peters roared.

With trembling hands, Stephanie Gash opened the three containers of barbecue sauce.

Father Peters turned off the torch and set it on the floor. He reached down with both hands and yanked at the meat covering McKayla's face.

Most of the skin on her skull came off with it. The girl kicked and writhed on the bed, the gleaming bone from her skull bright against the dark red of her muscles and blood.

Father Peters held the meat out to Stephanie Gash.

"Sauce me!" he yelled.

Stephanie clumsily dumped the barbecue sauce on the meat and Father Peters ate it so quickly it was like he was in some kind of competitive eating contest. His hunger abated and the room now seemed quiet.

The girl had stopped kicking. She'd stopped saying "Meat photo."

Stephanie Gash stood by the bed, shaking with sobs. "What . . . what did you do to her?"

Father Peters stifled a belch. "I removed the demon. His name was Alex. He's been around probably since 400 years before Christ or something."

"You killed her!"

"I removed the demon."

"She's dead."

"She will not be missed."

They both silently stared at the corpse of the young girl, Stephanie Gash in woeful sorrow and Father Peters with a sense of bold accomplishment. Then Father Peters heard a high-pitched shriek that sounded like it started in his head. His body exploded around the room, covering Stephanie Gash in gore. She began screaming. There was now a woman in the room.

Had she *come from* Father Peters?

"This can't be happening," Stephanie said.

"Meat photo!" the woman, nude except for a photo of meat on her face, roared.

Stephanie Gash turned to run and the woman swiped her to the floor. She picked up the torch, straddled Stephanie, and went to work.

# 35

**K**YLE THOUGHT HE'D MISSED HIS opportunity to finally kill Agnes and be free. He could have turned around and gone after her with the car. No one would have known. Opportunities like that did not present themselves every day. Now he was sad. Not even the feverish excitement in the air could break him out of his funk.

He missed Tony.

They'd had such good times together.

He pulled over to the side of the road and fished their favorite CD out of the glove compartment. He slid it into the car's CD player but it didn't work anymore so he just sat back and pretended to listen to the music that only played in his head and he thought about Tony. He missed the way he always smelled like cigarette smoke, mildew, and spoiled milk. That kid could talk about his mother for hours, how horrible she was. And Tony listened, really *listened* when Kyle needed to talk about Agnes or Chad. It was like Tony understood. Tony just got him. He wasn't sure he'd ever met another person who understood him so well.

Kyle glanced into his rearview mirror at the carts attached to his car, lying on their sides on the road. Guess he wouldn't be needing those anymore.

Tears streamed from his meat photo face. He didn't even bother wiping them away, just let them splash onto his bare chest. He looked at his meat photo mask in the mirror.

Was this who he was? Really?

He had no desire to take it off. It made him feel anonymous, yet unique. Maybe it was the thing that had been missing from his life.

He got out of the car, still a little weepy, and went around to the bumper. He began undoing the chains that had secured the carts to the car. He wouldn't be needing them now. It felt like a broken promise. The night was ending too early. He couldn't see himself going back to Tony's house. Not now, anyway. He didn't even know what he was thinking. It probably wouldn't have worked anyway. But, dammit, he and Tony would have had *so much fun* trying to make it work that it would have been totally worth it.

Now he was just a sad, middle-aged man in a meat photo mask.

How many people had he seen in masks just tonight? More than he could count.

How did he even compare?

He was nothing without Tony.

Once the carts were freed, he looked at his bounty in the backseat of the car.

All those meat photos.

All his.

Fair and square.

And how easily Tony had surrendered himself as payment. He didn't even *try* to resist. Kyle felt like he should have known it was over.

What would it take to get Tony back?

He wished he could cover himself in meat photos but he didn't have a glue stick or staples or anything.

He pulled one of the photos from the top of the stack and held it up to his face to lick it until he remembered the meat photo was covering his mouth. He rubbed the back of it against his mask and pressed it to his chest. Miraculously, it stayed in place. Kyle tugged at a corner to see how secure it was. He didn't think he could have pulled it off if he wanted to.

He continued sticking the photos to himself, thinking he was probably inventing the next big thing.

It took a while, but once he'd covered himself in every photo, all his sadness lifted. He felt reborn. If one Tony was the price for all these meat photos, then it felt like he was covered in Tony. That was logic.

He thought about getting back in his car and driving around but he didn't think he needed to. The car would feel too confining.

He sniffed the night air and looked up at the sky.

Then he saw the red light in the distance.

# 36

ANCIENT EVIL STOOD OUTSIDE, SMOKING a cigarette, listening to the sounds of the neighbors arguing. A dog in the house beside him was having another constant barking fit. The hum from the city wasn't enough to cover the cacophony of his neighborhood.

He was lost in his own thoughts as he smoked. The landlord was an asshole and told him he wasn't allowed to smoke in the house. He didn't see why it mattered. The place was run down and barely functional. It was all that he could afford after getting fired from the gallery.

Ancient Evil stubbed out his cigarette and tossed it in the metal coffee can he kept by the door. As he turned to go back inside so he could watch some more MeatTV and hope to finally fall asleep, something caught his eye.

A red beam of light shone into the night sky in the distance. The sight of the light seized him and something clicked in his head. He knew this was it. The Great Migration. The light was the sign he'd been waiting for his entire life. The excitement running through his body nearly made him wet himself. His heart raced with the anticipation and he ran inside to prepare himself.

He ran into the living room and stopped in front of "Meat Photo," which he'd hung above the inoperable fireplace years ago when he'd moved in. "It's time," he said and gently dismounted the photo. He held it at arm's length and took in its splendor one last time. The photo was magnificent and he knew the time had come to become one with it. But he remembered it wasn't enough and set it against the wall. He went to search for the smaller print he was certain he'd put in a filing cabinet in the attic.

He pulled the attic ladder down from the ceiling and climbed the rickety contraption. Once up the ladder he spotted the filing cabinet tucked into a corner and made his way to it, tossing all the other odds and ends he'd picked up over the years out of the way. A lot of the items broke but he didn't care. He reached the filing cabinet and pulled the top drawer open. The metal screamed in protest. The drawer was empty with the exception of the other print of meat he'd stolen from the gallery. He gently lifted the meat photo and went back down the stairs.

*There's something else I need*, he thought. He went to the kitchen and pulled open the junk drawer and pulled out the old roll of duct tape he kept there before returning to the living room.

The excitement he was feeling was greater than that of a little kid on Christmas morning. This was his life's work. This was why he was born. The Great Migration would be complete and he would be the ruler of the world.

He pulled a long strip of tape from the roll and attached it to the top of the print before affixing it over his face. He felt it conform to his face immediately and got a raging erection. This wouldn't do. The confines of this world were too much and he stripped off all his clothing. He felt better. He felt free. It all felt so natural to him. But his erection jutted straight out and he knew that would make the next step impossible. He grabbed his penis and masturbated with abandon. When he came, it shot onto the framed "Meat Photo" leaning against the wall. He thought this might ruin the photo but he didn't have time to clean it up. "Meat Photo" called to him and, to his surprise, his dick was still hard. He knew he didn't have time to jerk off again and picked up the large, framed artwork, flipped it so the photo was facing away from him, and thrust his cock into it. His erection was so powerful it penetrated the photo and he came a second time as it passed through. The framed photo covered his entire body and, even though it was held in place by his still-hard cock, he used some more duct tape to attach it to the front of him.

The photo came alive and he could feel it caressing his body and changing it and he couldn't stop orgasming, painting the walls of the living room with his semen. At some point, the pleasure too much, he collapsed.

When he woke, he could feel power surging through his veins. He'd changed. He was now fully Ancient Evil and would fulfill the prophecy. His arms felt like miles of linked sausage, flailing like tentacles, and his legs felt powerful, each like a large leg of lamb. He felt invincible and stepped outside to greet the world.

"Meat photo!" he bellowed into the night.

His battle cry was greeted by several howls from the neighborhood dogs and possibly a coyote. He lifted his head and spotted the red light in the night sky and took his first step toward his destiny.

# 37

**T**ONY AND NEAL DECIDED THE Dollar General was boring without all the photos of meat. They decided the best thing to do was to make their own entertainment. They scavenged around in the back room to see what had been left behind from the previous business.

"Holy fuck," Tony said. He lifted a display box of spray paint. "I'm gonna get so high." He immediately cracked open a can and began huffing it.

"What colors are those?" Neal asked.

Tony laughed. "Who fucking cares?"

Neal dug through the box and found the basic array of colors you could get from the Dollar General: red, black, white, and clear. "I have an idea."

"Good for you," Tony mocked him. "I'm smart and I have an idea."

Neal ignored him and took the box of spray paint back into the store. He immediately grabbed a can of red and a can of black and proceeded to paint the walls of the now empty store. It was difficult for him to see what he was doing in the red light but he let his creative juices flow.

Tony appeared from the back room with a small stereo and searched for a plug. Once he got the stereo working, he tuned it to the local dance music station and began dancing.

The fumes from Neal's spray painting were keeping Tony high and he was starting to feel a little sticky from the overspray. When a song ended, Tony stopped and looked at what Neal was doing.

"Whoa," Tony said. "Is that . . ." He was still high from huffing and dizzy from dancing and having a hard time putting words together.

"Meat," Neal said. "Your dad—"

"Who?"

"The guy that traded you for all the photos."

"Don't think he's my dad."

"He took my life's work. But I can do something else to replace it all. I'm going to cover the walls with paintings of meat. One continuous meat mural. The Dollar General will become one building-size meat photo, inside and out."

"That's . . . awesome," Tony slurred and lit a cigarette. Another song had started and Tony began to dance again. After a few seconds he stopped. "Oh! Oh! I just had the best idea ever. We should turn this place into a club. A meat club. Only people with meat photos can get in. A dance club. Club Meat."

"Look, you can do whatever you want, but I got a lot of painting to do."

"Old people are so fucking boring."

"I'm not even thirty."

"Yeah, old."

"Fuck off. Go start your dance club or whatever."

Tony, high out of his mind, wandered out of the Dollar General. He stood outside and lit three more cigarettes, plugging them into the meat on his face and puffing away. He didn't really have any idea how one started a dance club. They had music. He felt like that was a pretty good start. He drifted out into the parking lot in a cloud of smoke and spray-paint fumes and looked back at the store, thinking, *Club Meat*. He had a teacher at school who'd always told him he should think more positively.

He imagined the Dollar General packed with people, all semi-naked and wearing meat photo masks. Once people heard about it, he knew they would flock to it.

Then he noticed the red light shooting up from the roof of the Dollar General.

It must be a sign.

He was suddenly aroused.

He made his way back into the store. He could no longer contain himself. He went to a darkened corner and began furiously masturbating. He'd done this quite a bit but never to complete fruition. He'd watched tons of porn, so he knew what was supposed to happen, but he'd always gotten distracted before he could make himself ejaculate. Plus, sometimes his penis became too raw and sore. But he felt like this would be the day.

Then he felt a sensation in his lower stomach and balls he'd never felt before. His penis became stiffer than ever and he finally shot his load with a scream.

Neal came running out of the back room.

"What the fuck's going on?" he said.

Tony, staring down at his emission, said, "Nobody told me it was supposed to hurt."

Neal, totally confused, scratched his head and said, "I don't . . . It's not supposed to?"

They both looked down at Tony's first ejaculation. This was not a normal expulsion.

Tony had ejaculated a wad of meat that lay writhing on the floor.

"This means something," Neal said.

Tony, pulling up his underwear, said, "I think I need to dance."

# 38

**T**YLER THOUGHT HE WAS ONTO some pretty next-level shit. Ever since graduating high school, he'd been really into wigs. He'd accumulated so many of them that it became a problem. His mom, an abusive alcoholic with a goiter, had told him he had to get a place of his own. She'd never understood his enthusiasm for wigs, always reminding him that she'd given him a headful of glorious hair. Which was true. But it wasn't the hair he wanted. And it was too much work to maintain. With the wigs, he could just keep his head shaved and put on whichever he wanted every day. Hell, he could wear, like, a whole lot of wigs a day if he wanted to. Hair didn't grow that fast. You got a haircut and you were stuck with it for however long it took to grow back. Plus, you could dye it whatever color you wanted to, maybe, but you couldn't do that all the time or you'd fry it.

Lately, however, he'd found himself more into meat photos than wigs. He liked putting them on his face and wearing them like a mask. He'd been doing this the last couple of days. He'd seen a few other people doing it online and wasn't sure if he'd started the trend or was just following the trend. It didn't matter. What mattered was that he enjoyed doing it. Ever since, he'd had moments where he didn't even think about putting on a wig.

Tonight, however, he'd discovered the joy of putting wigs on his meat photos.

The first time he'd done it, he'd muttered, "Perfection," and immediately masturbated three times in rapid succession.

Now all of his meat photos were also wearing wigs. Tyler himself was wearing a meat photo and three wigs. He'd never so much as doubled up on the wigs before and felt like he'd missed a great opportunity. Sure, his head was kind of hot, but the meat photo seemed to drink the sweat pouring from his head.

He admired himself in the large mirror he kept in the middle of the living room. Who needed a TV when you had a giant mirror you could stare at yourself in?

As he looked at himself, admiring the way the locks of the wigs draped over the meat photo mask, he thought about what everyone was talking about online.

The Great Migration, they were calling it.

Most people didn't seem to know where they were migrating to. Some of them mentioned a red beam in the sky.

He stepped out onto his balcony as a palate cleanser. To continue enjoying staring at himself in the mirror, he occasionally needed to step away and look at something else. Out on the balcony, he could only really think about getting back to the mirror.

And he thought he saw it.

This couldn't be real.

Out on the edge of town, he swore he saw a powerful beam of red light shooting up into the sky.

He thought it was out where the old Dollar General was.

This seemed too good to be true.

He'd had no real plans of joining the Great Migration because he thought it sounded really far away. Nothing ever happened in his town. Now, seeing that it was so close, he felt like he had to take part in it.

He had another idea. If he were to take his bewigged meat photos, he could probably manage to make enough money to pay rent.

Excited, he rushed back into his apartment.

A man stood in the middle of his living room.

The door seemed undisturbed and Tyler had no idea how this man had gotten in.

Unfortunately, this kind of thing happened to Tyler quite a bit. There had been at least four times he'd woken up to other people in his apartment. Most of them were just kind of confused, like they thought maybe they were in their apartment. Only one of them had seemed upset and administered a quick but effective beating Tyler had recovered from after only a couple of days.

He thought he knew how to handle the situation.

"I like your mask, dude," Tyler said. "You want to try a wig. I have a ton."

"Meat photo," the man said.

Tyler was now pretty sure the man was covered in blood but was only slightly alarmed. He was probably just a butcher or a surgeon or something. Not everything had a complicated explanation. Rationality and simplicity was always the best answer.

The man moved on Tyler with surprising speed and agility.

Tyler went limp. He'd learned this technique from his previous beating. It was best just to play dead or unconscious or something. The last guy had gotten bored pretty quickly before stealing everything in Tyler's refrigerator and moving on.

The man forced Tyler's mouth open, stripped off one of his wigs, and shoved it into Tyler's mouth. Tyler had to fight back his gag reflex as the man continued shoving the wig down his throat. Tyler began thinking maybe he'd have to go to the hospital to have the wig removed before joining up with the Great Migration. Then the man grabbed the second wig from Tyler's head and began shoving that in too.

Now Tyler couldn't breathe and started getting a little panicked. He tried to tell the guy he couldn't breathe but he couldn't form the words. Soon, he felt himself losing consciousness and, in a last-ditch effort to save his life, took a weak swipe at the man shoving wigs down his throat.

It didn't help.

# 39

**A**GNES HAD WANDERED INTO A part of town even more rundown than the area she lived. She felt like she was floating on a cloud and her own thoughts came back to her. The meat photo had taken over but now it was just guiding her. She'd never had such clearly defined goals. She didn't know what she would do once she finally reached the red light, but that was for fate to decide. It was something she didn't want to think too much about.

She moved through a dark, narrow alley that smelled like cat piss. Most of the security lamps were broken and the alley was very dark.

A man moved into the alley in front of her, stopping Agnes in her tracks.

This was the most gorgeous man she'd ever seen. He had the most beautiful photo of meat duct taped around his head. But what really made the man so striking was the larger photo of meat affixed to his torso. She couldn't be sure since the lighting was bad but she thought the man's large photo had a penis jutting from it.

"You're very beautiful," she said.

"My name is Ancient Evil," the man said.

"I'm Agnes Baker," she said, holding out her hand. She felt sure this man was undoubtedly a gentleman and would take her proffered hand and hold it up to his mouth in the sweetest kiss she would ever feel.

The man took her hand and yanked her frail body close to him. She could feel his large cock pressing against her and knew he was attracted to her.

Before she knew it, he was pulling her into the large meat photo on his torso.

Agnes had only a brief second of panic before relenting to the feel of actual meat wrapping itself around her body. She didn't know how any of this was possible. Her world went completely dark but she knew where she was. She was inside this man who'd called himself Ancient Evil. She was now a part of him. No longer was she the old sick and diseased Agnes Baker. Now she was going to be part of something the likes of which the world had never seen. She'd never felt more special or chosen in her life.

When the man started moving with her somewhere deep inside him, she knew he was going to take her to her destination.

This, she knew, was the man who would lead the Great Migration.

# 40

**K**YLE GUESSED HE WAS STILL about a mile away from the red light. All the meat photos attached to his body made him feel powerful and secure.

"I'm coming for you, Tony!" he shouted into the night.

He was sure he would have to battle Neal for the right to win Tony back. Returning the meat photos was not an option. Kyle wanted it all. He wanted Tony and he wanted all the meat photos. Maybe he could work out a payment plan with Neal.

As he walked along in the dark, he thought about all the good times he and Tony had had. Kyle wept loudly as he made his way toward the red light. He bawled and screamed so much it almost took until he'd walked up on the commotion before he realized what was happening.

A large group of people were protesting outside the metal fence surrounding the slaughterhouse. People with signs marched in a circle chanting, "Meat is murder!" while pumping shitty homemade signs up and down. They seemed angrier than any other time he'd driven past the slaughterhouse.

The lights in the parking lot of the slaughterhouse weren't the greatest but Kyle could see people running in and out of the building.

107

They were working in teams to carry large, skinned cow carcasses toward something in the middle of the parking lot. Kyle wanted to get a better look but he was slightly afraid of the protesters. He knew they would never understand how important his photos of meat were and they would probably try to rip them off his body and destroy his suit.

He heard an unearthly scream and noticed whatever the people were running toward seemed to be growing. That's when he realized what was happening. The people were running toward someone with an extremely large photo of meat strapped to themselves. He was certain the person had ripped a hole in the photo and their erection was exposed. Kyle could understand the man's excitement. Just looking at the enormous meat photo made Kyle hard.

The people carrying the carcasses all wore meat photos as masks and when they got close to the man they were being sucked into the photo. Each person and cow carcass that was absorbed into the photo made the man and his photo a little bit bigger.

The photo absorbing the people was so beautiful Kyle wanted to be a part of it but he was also very jealous of it. He wanted the photo. He wanted to wear the photo. It made his suit of meat photos feel inadequate and that made Kyle angry.

"Hey, asshole!" someone shouted from the group of protesters. "Meat is murder!"

Kyle turned around just in time to see the open bucket sailing through the air, trailing red paint as it soared straight toward his face. The bucket exploded upon impact, causing Kyle's face to erupt in blinding hot pain. He heard the crunch of his nose and felt most of his teeth shatter as he fell to the ground. If he hadn't been so ensconced in the pain and anger of knowing his meat photo suit was ruined he would've heard the crowd of protesters cheering at his humiliation.

Once his senses came back to him, Kyle realized the group of protesters had surrounded him and were berating him.

"Change what you eat! Change the world!"

"Peace starts on your plate!"

"Love animals! Eat veggies!"

Kyle could feel the red paint covering his beautiful photos and rage filled every fiber of his being. He reached out and grabbed the ankle of the closest protester, a girl in a flowing skirt with bleached dreadlocks, and pulled her off her feet. Her head hit the pavement with a sickening thud and instantly cracked open like a smashed pumpkin. The other protesters backed up and froze as Kyle got to his feet.

"Murderer!" one of them shouted.

"Meat photo!" Kyle bellowed.

He grabbed both ankles of the fallen protester and spun in circles to club down the whole group. Kyle proceeded to beat the protesters to death before carrying each one toward the growing man and chucking them into the ever-growing photo. Once they were all absorbed, he stood in front of the towering man and stared at the beautiful photo.

"I'm Ancient Evil," the man said.

"Uh-huh," Kyle said, not knowing what else to say. "Meat photo."

Kyle felt his body being pulled toward the photo and could do nothing to stop it. He thought he should resist it but knew he would be a part of something much larger if he gave in. He thought about Tony and how much he wanted to find him again but something told him if he gave in that what he would be rewarded with would be much better than what he and Tony had.

"Meat photo," Kyle said.

"Yes," Ancient Evil said. "Meat photo."

Kyle went slack as he was pulled into Ancient Evil's photo. It was warm inside and it smelled just like meat.

# 41

**T**ABITHA LOOKED AT THE GLAMOUR Shots flyer again. "Get your photo taken with meat!" was at the top, followed by several hazy photos of women surrounded by artfully arranged meat. Each of the women wore a pound of makeup, skimpy clothing, and their hair had been curled and teased to make them look like soap stars from the 80s. Beside one photo was the caption, "My husband loves the way I look with all this meat. He hung it above our fireplace!" There was another headline that read, "Give your boyfriend a sexy photo of you with prime cuts!"

At the bottom of the flyer was the address of the photo studio and a disclaimer that you could get one 8-inch by 10-inch photo for just twenty dollars if you brought the flyer to the studio. It also boasted that it was open twenty-four hours a day, which she found odd but convenient. Tabitha didn't have a boyfriend or a husband but she thought twenty dollars was really cheap for a great looking photo of herself. She thought she could use it as a profile photo on a dating site. Meat photos seemed to be all the rage lately and surely she'd snag a guy with a sexy photo like the ones displayed on the flyer. She'd found the flyer under the windshield wiper of her car after leaving an Arby's a few days earlier. And maybe her future husband would hang the photo above their fireplace so he could admire the beautiful woman he'd married.

Tabitha pulled open the door to Glamour Shots. A bell dinged a few times to alert someone that a customer had arrived. The waiting room was empty but she could hear voices coming from the back. She looked down a hallway and spotted a flash of light.

"Just finishing up!" someone called. "Be right there!"

"Okay," Tabitha responded.

Tabitha thought about taking a seat but chose to stand instead, inspecting all the beautiful photos of women surrounded by meat. Eventually two women appeared from the back, one telling the other that she would get a call in a few days to review her photos before the customer left.

The remaining woman looked at her and grimaced slightly. "My name's Mary. Welcome to Glamour Shots. Can I help you?"

Tabitha held out the flyer. "Says I can get a photo for twenty dollars."

"Ah. Yes. Umm."

"You can make me sexy?"

"Uh. Well. Let's see what we can do. Follow me."

Tabitha followed Mary down the hallway and into a small room filled with outfits and all the things that would be needed to do someone's makeup and hair. A disgruntled looking woman thumbed her phone screen but didn't look up.

"Got another for ya, Amy," Mary said.

Amy looked up at Tabitha. "Are you fucking kidding me?"

Mary sighed. "Let me know when she's ready." She promptly left the room.

Tabitha said, "I wanna look sexy."

"Sit," Amy barked and pointed to a chair.

Tabitha did as she was told and Amy got to work on her hair. It didn't take as long as Tabitha thought it would. Her hair was huge and beautiful.

Amy picked up a makeup brush and scrutinized Tabitha's face before dropping the tool. "Let's try something different." She pulled open a drawer on the vanity and retrieved a photo of meat before picking up a headband from the vanity top. She held the photo of meat over Tabitha's face and placed the headband over it to affix it there.

"I can't see anything," Tabitha said.

"Shut up," Amy said.

"I want to look sexy."

"This is the new thing. It's sexy."

"But how will people know it's me?"

"You ask too many questions. I'm the makeup artist here. Just do what I tell you. I'm doing you a favor because there is no amount of makeup and soft lighting in the world to make you look attractive."

Tabitha felt disappointed but she thought about how the photo was going to cost twenty dollars and knew she was only getting what she paid for. Maybe if she'd splurged and bought one of their packages they would've made her sexy.

Amy barked, "Take off your shirt and bra."

"Why?"

"Just do what I tell you."

Tabitha did as she was told. Amy wrapped a putrid green feather boa around her shoulders and breasts.

"There," Amy said. "Now go to the next door on the right to have your photo taken."

"But I don't like green and I wanted a full body photo. Can't I get a pink boa?" She remembered seeing the pink boa on the rack with all the other assortment of colored boas.

"No, you can't use the pink one. And honey, we're doing you a favor by not taking a full body photo."

This was not at all the experience Tabitha wanted. She'd hoped to go to Arby's afterward and sit in the dining room with her new hair and professional makeup. Maybe a guy would notice how beautiful and sexy she was and take her out on a date, possibly to another Arby's.

"Well . . . do I at least get to pick the cuts of meat I'm photographed with?"

"You can, yeah. But that'll cost extra. And, let me be honest with you, you look like a flank steak kind of girl so there probably isn't a point in paying extra. Of course, everybody wants the filet mignon or the Wagyu because it's the most expensive, but those are just gonna make you look even bigger."

Tabitha thought this would be more of a luxury experience. She didn't feel very pampered. This woman was making her feel like trash. She had never been fat shamed by an employee before.

Tabitha didn't want to because she hated confrontation, but she took a deep breath and said, "I am going to leave a such a bad review for you."

Amy snorted laughter and said, "Honey, you're at one of the last remaining Glamour Shots at three in the morning to have your picture taken with meat. Do you really think any review you could leave is going to hurt us?"

The woman had a point and, in a way, her saying this was even more devastating than the fat shaming. She was right. There was nothing Tabitha could do to hurt this woman who'd clearly been damaged by something much more traumatic at an earlier point in her life.

Tabitha huffed and made her way to the next door, tripping over something in the process and nearly falling down. It was difficult for her to see with the meat photo on her face. She tilted her head back to see if she could see out from under the photo.

The photographer was messing with a camera and smoking a cigarette. Tabitha coughed and fanned her face. She thought about putting that in her future bad review but knew it would probably only end up making them look cooler and edgy and would end up attracting a whole other type of consumer. Sort of like the people who move to Las Vegas so they can smoke everywhere they go.

"All right," the photographer said. "Go stand in front of the backdrop."

The backdrop was a photo of depressing factories. Just to the right of the backdrop was a wheelbarrow with a lot of flies buzzing around it. It was weird. The longer she wore the meat photo, the better she could see through it.

"Don't I get to at least pick the background? There's nothing sexy about industrial wastelands."

"You can, but it costs extra. Besides, industrial wastelands are super sexy. Now get up there and grab you some meat out of that wheelbarrow."

Tabitha really didn't think it would be up to her to artfully arrange the meat. This whole experience was so . . . discount. What did she expect? She felt like crying. She couldn't wait to get out of this place. She'd stop by Waffle House and order a lot of food and talk to that toothless guy who was always there and maybe play some sad songs on the jukebox. She was pretty sure Arby's would be closed.

"Can we get this over with?" the photographer said. "I'm already supposed to be on break."

Tabitha trundled up to the backdrop. She reached into the wheelbarrow and grabbed a couple handfuls of meat and held them out to the photographer like, "Tell me what to do with these."

"Just put 'em on your shoulders or tits or something. Maybe you should put one over your face if you're going to try and use it on one of those dating sites. Men love girls whose faces look like meat. It's mysterious." Tabitha didn't know if this was true or not. The meat had clearly gone rancid and the thought of putting it on her face repulsed her. But she had to remind herself that she was here to try and snag a man. This other woman had probably photographed hundreds if not thousands of people and part of Tabitha thought maybe she should listen to her.

"But I already have a photo of meat on my face."

The photographer shrugged. "It's probably best if you double up."

"I just don't want to be accused of catfishing."

She rested a cut of meat on her head, letting it drape down like bangs. She didn't want to cover the photo of meat on her face, afraid she'd have to pay if it got ruined. There was something oddly comforting about it. She put a couple more cuts on her shoulders, thinking maybe it would make them look a little less broad. Finally, she took a thinner cut of meat and tucked it into the waistband of her underwear.

"Perfect," the photographer said. "Wait a minute."

The photographer grabbed a spray bottle and approached Tabitha. She covered Tabitha in a cold mist.

"This is so you look real sweaty," the photographer said. "Guys like sweaty girls. Plus it makes the meat glisten better. Gives it that shine."

The photographer moved back behind the camera while Tabitha stood cold, wet, and covered with meat, trying to strike moderately seductive poses.

She became distracted by something else.

Heavy breathing came from somewhere behind her. At first, she thought it was maybe a sound being piped in through the studio, although she couldn't understand why they'd want to do anything to make the vibe even creepier.

She got down in a squat to really accentuate the meat hanging down between her legs, tried smiling in her most sensuous manner although it was hidden by the mask, and jumped when she heard the backdrop behind her rip.

The camera continued to flash relentlessly as Tabitha turned to see a woman wearing a photo of artfully arranged meat as a mask. The masked woman grabbed each end of the boa and yanked it tightly around her neck. Tabitha struggled to get away, thinking the boa was probably not of the highest quality and would easily break. But the woman continued pulling on it until it began to cut into Tabitha's thick neck. She tried to scream but her vocal cords were severed and her head came off, a geyser of blood spraying the shredded backdrop.

The photographer continued snapping photos.

# 42

E ARLIER THAT DAY, MACKENZIE HAD made plans to kill her boyfriend, Skully. He was the biggest asshole she'd ever met. She couldn't believe she'd let him move in with her. He'd only been here for a couple of weeks and that was two weeks too long. She'd asked him to move out a few days ago but he'd just stared at her, dead-eyed. Her main problem with him was that he was so lazy. Shortly after moving in with her, he'd stripped off all his clothes and lain in her bed. He didn't even bring anything with him. Said he only ate like once every two weeks. He did nothing but lie in bed, sometimes changing his position. He didn't even use the bathroom. He'd just shit wherever he was. And whenever Mackenzie would enter the room to remove his waste or just check on him, he would become unnecessarily hostile and aggressive toward her. Once, he'd even tried to bite her. His latest kick was saying he wanted to remove his arms and legs.

"I don't need 'em," he'd said. "I'll just learn to slither if I ever have to move."

She'd never known a bigger asshole.

She had gathered all the knives from the kitchen. She planned on opening the door to her bedroom (well, she guessed it was Skully's bedroom now) and throwing the knives at him. She thought she had enough of them to do the trick.

But now, looking at the knives, she felt like she'd had a change of plans. She'd just watched a YouTube video on something called the Great Migration. People were flocking to a red beam coming out of an old Dollar General on the edge of town. She'd felt so alone her whole life. Being around other like-minded people, the meat photo people, sounded exactly like something she wanted to do. She wished her bedroom locked from the outside so she could trap Skully in there, leaving him to starve to death on his own.

She sighed and looked out her window at the red beam in the distance. Now was not the time to have vindictive thoughts. Once she left her house and was on her way to join the Great Migration, she would be free from him. She'd be free from everything.

~

Marla couldn't remember when she'd affixed the photo of artfully arranged meat to her face, but her life had improved dramatically ever since. So much so that she was pretty sure she didn't need her children anymore. This thought had occurred to her only a few moments ago and she'd gone to wake her two kids up. They hadn't even started kindergarten yet, so they were still pretty dumb. She took each of their hands and walked them over to her neighbor's house. Callie seemed tired when she came to the door but not surprised to see her. Callie was one of the few women in the neighborhood who hadn't yet found a photo of artfully arranged meat to put on her face. Marla didn't know if it was because she was somehow morally opposed to it or if she was just lazy.

"They're yours now," Marla said.

"What's mine?" Callie said.

"The kids. I'm off to join the Great Migration."

"The Great . . . ?"

"You wouldn't understand. You're one of the naked ones." Marla didn't say them, but she thought other words like: *Infidel. Sinner. Unclean.*

"I guess a couple more isn't going to make a difference. It's becoming like a goddamn orphanage in here."

Marla didn't care enough to look into Callie's house but if she had, she would've seen a number of children of various ages sleeping on the floor in her living room.

"Thanks," Marla said. "It really means a lot."

Then she turned to walk back to the sidewalk. Her young daughter

(Marla had already forgotten her name) said, "Mommy?"

Marla flipped her off and continued walking toward the red beam.

~

Ryan was really excited as he scrolled through his phone. Mark continued melting down the Nerds Rope on the stove. He laughed loudly and shouted, "This is just how I prefer them!" He said this every time he melted down a Nerds Rope on the stove. Ryan guessed it was a quirk he thought others would find interesting but it had just grown tedious.

Both of them wore meat photos.

Ryan rushed up to Mark, brandishing his phone.

"Dude," Ryan said. "We're joining the Great Migration."

"What the fuck is that?!" Mark shouted.

"I just heard about it on Twitter. It's trending. And now it's my favorite thing ever."

"I thought meat photos were the best thing ever!"

"Calm down, bro. They are. But get this. The Great Migration is only for people like us. The meat photo people. We're global, baby!"

"Fuck yeah!"

"So you're in?"

"I'm so in!" Mark celebrated by lifting the pan of liquified Nerds Rope and chugging it down.

They went out into the night to follow the red beam. They didn't bother shutting the door behind them. They knew they wouldn't be coming back.

~

Shelly wasn't sure if the meat photo was making her happy anymore. Sure, it had opened doors for her since she'd first put it on. Her life had really changed for the better. But the last few hours had been pretty disappointing. The thrill was gone. She'd spent an hour or so shopping for new meat photo masks online. She found one she liked but the retailer only accepted cryptocurrency and she didn't know what that was or how to use it. So she had decided to get into her car and drive as fast as she could until she hit something that would hopefully kill her or at least make her life more exciting.

She had all the windows down and had reached a speed of well over a hundred when she heard about the Great Migration on the radio. She slammed on the brakes until she'd brought the car to a stop. She bolted out of the car and sniffed the air like a feral animal. She smelled meat. Delicious, succulent, raw meat.

And she saw the light. A thick red beam shooting straight up into the air.

A couple of teenagers in meat photo masks were stumbling up the sidewalk.

"Are you guys part of the Great Migration?" Shelly called to them.

"Meat photo," one of the teens said.

"Meat photo," the other teen said.

"Meat photo," Shelly said, and by that she meant, "I'm going to join you."

~

Jake had spent all day uploading some photos of meat to his computer. He'd spent the previous night on Reddit and everyone was raving about how much money he could make selling NFTs. The concept was a little abstract at first but he finally got his head wrapped around it.

The thought of being able to quit his job and never work again by taking a handful of photos and uploading them to the internet kept Jake up all night. In the early morning he'd driven to a meat market and bought everything he could afford, which wasn't much. But he knew it was an investment. If he cleaned out his savings now, he would be a millionaire in a couple of days. The people on Reddit were talking about how much money they'd made by just taking photos of meat, which they in turn sold to people so they could make the photos into masks. Jake wasn't into trendy things but apparently meat photos were all the rage.

Jake had been awake ever since. He'd called into work and told them he wouldn't be coming back and spent the rest of the day and into the next night working as quickly as he could. He found he had to spend even more money to get the NFTs listed and maxed out his credit card.

Once everything was done, he went back over to the Reddit thread to see how other people were doing with their NFTs, but everything had changed. No one was talking about NFTs anymore. It was all about something called the Great Migration. People were saying it was going to be *everything* and NFTs were so yesterday. They kept talking about a red light that could be seen and people were signing off to go to its source.

Jake walked to his living room window and peered outside. He could see the light and it thrilled him. He knew he had to go to it. He didn't know why but he knew that if he did he'd never have to work again.

He grabbed one of the photos he'd taken early in the day and cut holes in the sides so he could slip his ears in them to keep it on his face. He left the house and started walking toward the red light.

~

"Dude," Tim said. "We did it!" He held up his hand toward Bill. "High five!"

Bill gave him a high five. "Holy shit! I can't believe it! Meat Coin is live!"

"People are gonna buy the shit out of it! It's a better meme coin than Doge!"

"Yeah, fuck that stupid dog! We're gonna be so rich!"

Tim and Bill hugged each other and started frottaging. They both had boners. Neither one of them cared. They were both excited at the prospect of being the founders of Meat Coin, the newest crypto-currency.

Bill said, "We need to get a hold of every business that sells photos of meat and convince them that people should only buy their photos with Meat Coin."

Tim took out his phone and started looking for businesses. All he could find was information about the Great Migration and something called Club Meat. There was a ton of buzz about the club. It appeared a lot of people with meat photo masks were heading there tonight.

"Have you seen this?" Tim said.

Bill was staring off into space and absentmindedly rubbing his cock. "Huh? See what?"

Tim offered Bill his phone. "Club Meat. It's new and everyone with a meat photo mask is headed there right now. Or already there."

"It's like . . ." Bill looked at the time on Tim's phone. "It's nearly four in the morning, dude. There's no way that place is still open."

Tim took his phone back from Bill. "It says it's open twenty-four hours." He thumbed through Instagram and watched a few videos of people dancing.

"So?"

"We should go. We could get the word out about Meat Coin. Maybe talk a bunch of people into buying it. Maybe even talk the club owner into making it the official and only way to pay to get into the club or whatever."

"Dude, that's fucking brilliant."

"Says to follow the red light after you step outside."

"Well, what are we waiting for?"

"Grab your meat photo and let's go."

~

Carol read about the Great Migration in the Facebook group called Meat Lovers. She spent most of her days on Facebook, but more specifically, in the Meat Lovers group. Her husband, Thomas, never paid much attention to her anymore, more interested in watching whatever sport he could find on television. The other women at her office job started wearing photos of meat as masks a couple of days ago and Carol had felt left out. So on her way home that day she stopped at a gas station and bought one for herself before heading home. Thomas had ridiculed her for it but he was just being an old fuddy-duddy. He didn't understand they were both getting older and Carol was determined to stay relevant with the younger crowd.

Eventually, he'd just mumbled "Sport" and gone back to his man cave.

The next day at work the women had started raving about the Meat Lovers group on Facebook. Carol had Facebook but was still really confused about how it worked or why she even had it. She only had five friends and they only seemed to post pictures of themselves and argue about politics. Carol figured out how to search for the group and sent a request that was accepted immediately. The quick acceptance made Carol feel validated. She'd obsessively check the group and there was always something new posted there.

Carol couldn't stop looking at the Meat Lovers group. Now she lay in bed next to Thomas as he snored away, wearing her meat photo, and scrolling through the posts she'd already read through earlier that day. The posts seemed to slow down a bit after people began posting about the Great Migration.

A new post popped up in the timeline with a photo. The photo was of the night sky and a red beam of light. The caption read, "The Great Migration! I'm headed there now. If you're not going then no one cares about you and you should probably kill yourself."

"Oh no," Carol said.

Thomas snorted in his sleep and it grated on Carol's nerves. She kicked him in the leg but he kept on snoring. She needed to get to the Great Migration and just knew the other women from the office were probably already there. They'd be talking about how great it was to-morrow and it would make Carol feel like an outsider. Carol couldn't have that but she knew if she were to get out of bed it would wake up Thomas and he would tell her how stupid she was being and to go back to bed and stop fucking around on Facebook all the time.

Carol pulled the pillow from behind her head. She placed it over Thomas' snoring face and lay on top of his head. Thomas flailed around, probably more confused about waking up to being smothered more than anything, and gave up quickly. Carol continued to lie on the pillow until Thomas hadn't moved for what felt like five minutes.

She slipped out of bed, got dressed, and stepped outside. The red beam of light was bright in the night sky and she saw a lot of other people walking down the street, wearing photos of meat on their faces, and heading toward the light. Carol joined them.

# 43

ANCIENT EVIL KNEW HE WAS close to the red light's source but he was tired of walking and thought it would be quicker if he drove. He didn't have a car but spotted someone's phone lying in the parking lot of the slaughterhouse and picked it up. Thankfully whoever had dropped it hadn't had a passcode and they also had the Uber app. He pulled up the app and ordered a car.

A beat-up Nissan Versa arrived a few minutes later. Ancient Evil had absorbed so many people and so much meat it was difficult for him to fit in the back seat of the car. He had to spread his legs wide and let the framed photo sit on the floor.

The driver looked at his phone, a bit confused, and back at Ancient Evil. "Your destination is only half a mile away."

"Yeah, man, I'm way too . . . bulky to walk that far."

"I'm not complainin'. You goin' to that place with the red light too. I took a lotta people there tonight. A *lot*." The guy pulled onto the road. "Traffic's gettin' pretty crazy. Must be nice to just hang out and party all night. I gotta drive this car so I can buy my daughter some teeth and a new knee."

Ancient Evil didn't say anything.

The Uber driver reached back and put his hand on Ancient Evil's thigh. "What about you? You like to party?" The driver glanced at Ancient Evil's dick protruding through the hole in the enormous photo.

Ancient Evil could barely feel the hand on his thigh. His skin was stretched too tight.

"I don't really remember what I like to do. All I know is that I'm very powerful. I'm the reason all the people are going there."

The Uber driver quickly took his hand away. "I knew you was one of them freaks. Overnight, everybody just starts wearing photos of meat on their faces. I can't even afford a picture of meat. Probably couldn't afford a picture of beans. What the fuck do I care? Probably makes 'em look better. That's what they should call that club of yours. Club Butterface. No judgments at Club Butterface."

Ancient Evil cleared his throat and said, "Their day of judgment is near. They will all be judged by the meat they wear upon their faces. There is one photo of meat that doesn't belong. It's the one that needs to be destroyed."

"Sheesh," the Uber driver said. "You ain't goin' there to shoot up the place, are ya?"

Ancient Evil didn't answer right away.

The driver said, "Eh, I guess it ain't none of my business anyway."

There was a line of traffic leading to the Dollar General. Because there were no cars coming from the opposite direction, the driver swerved over into that lane and sped toward Club Meat.

"Figure you're an important guy and I don't want to keep your fans waiting," the driver said.

Ancient Evil didn't understand sarcasm or much of anything so he had to take the driver at his word. Still, he was thankful the driver hadn't made him wait through the line.

"Would you like to join us?" Ancient Evil asked.

"Well, sure, I'd love to, but as I already stated, I gotta keep drivin' 'cause of my defective daughter and I ain't got no meat mask. Plus, eventually I'll find someone who'll trade a blowjob or at least a handjob for the fare. My wife sewed her pussy shut. Pees through a tube. Did it out of spite."

All of this meant nothing to Ancient Evil. He grunted and thought he expelled something from his anus. He reached back between his buttocks and pulled a fresh new meat photo out of his ass.

"Here is your meat photo." Ancient Evil presented the photo to the driver.

The driver held it up to his face and said, "I just do it like that?"

124

Without any type of tape or fastener, the photo adhered to the driver's face, forming perfectly to his contours.

The driver arrived at the Dollar General and stopped in front of the door. Ancient Evil got out of the car. The Uber driver pulled his car into a handicap spot in the packed parking lot and got out.

Ancient Evil approached the driver, spread his arms, and absorbed him into a world Ancient Evil hoped he would never experience.

Then he approached Club Meat in search of the false mask.

# 44

**F**ROM A CONDO IN WEST Hollywood, Nicolas Cage scrolled through a Reddit thread about how much some people hated his face and he cried through the veil of his meat photo mask. He couldn't understand why the internet was such a cruel place. These people weren't even talking about how much they hated his movies. Some of them seemed to like them quite a bit. They were specifically talking about how much they hated his face. They didn't say he was ugly or malformed. Most of them didn't even know what it was specifically. He kept reading and weeping and was seriously considering giving up on acting altogether. He'd often thought about moving to the Midwest and getting into data entry. They could put him in the corner, somewhere where nobody would have to look at his face. He'd change his name to something like Dan Banal and wear a lot of unflattering clothes. Then he figured people in the office would probably start referring to him as Dan Anal or something, even though it wasn't pronounced that way. He'd have to think of another name.

The balcony door slid open and disrupted him from his self-loathing. Keanu Reeves peeked his head in the door and said, "Dude, you gotta come and look at this."

Nicolas Cage sighed and closed the tabs on his old laptop. The other tab he had open was a Reddit thread of people talking about how much they loved Keanu Reeves. Most of them didn't even like his movies, they just got a good "vibe" from the guy. He'd moved in with Keanu only a few short months ago. The guy hardly even worked. Nicolas Cage had made ten movies since he'd been living there and Keanu had only even read like two scripts.

"Coming." Nicolas Cage stood up and followed Keanu Reeves out to the cheap, wooden balcony.

Keanu Reeves pointed dramatically into the distance. "You see it?"

Nicolas Cage squinted and looked toward the horizon.

Keanu sighed.

"What?" Nicolas Cage said.

"Nothing. I just hate it when you make that face."

"You can't see my face. I'm wearing a meat photo."

"I'm wearing a meat photo too, so it reads through."

"Sorry, dude, it's just my face. I can't do anything about it."

"You can't *afford* to do anything about it, you mean," Keanu Reeves said.

"You can be a real dick sometimes. What the fuck am I supposed to be seeing?"

Keanu Reeves again dramatically pointed to the eastern horizon.

"Whoa!" Nicolas Cage said. "I just read about that on the computer. I didn't think I'd be able to see it all the way out here."

"It's time," Keanu Reeves said. "This is what we've been waiting for."

"If you can pay for a plane, I can get us there. I learned how to drive one in *Con-Air*."

"Drive?"

"Drive, fly, whatever. I can do it."

"I'll call my plane guy," Keanu Reeves said.

Nicolas Cage was already bristling with the excitement of going to the Midwest.

# 45

**T**ONY HAD NEVER FELT THIS good in his life. What he was experiencing didn't feel like a dream because he'd never dreamt of anything this great before. Actually, most of his dreams had been anxiety-fueled nightmares about being buried alive in his mother's towering hoard. But now he could only imagine being buried in meat and sweaty human flesh.

The club was packed.

There were flashing lights and music and everyone wore meat photos as masks and people were only wearing their underwear, if they wore any clothing at all.

Soon, he knew, these people would move outside the club and they would start their own clubs and it wouldn't be long before there were Club Meats all over the world and he would control all of them.

Normally, he only thought about smoking, huffing, getting generally fucked up, and hanging out with Kyle, so he didn't know where these thoughts were coming from. Probably the meat adhered to his face. He didn't care. He was young. There would still be plenty of time for him to do all that other stuff. If he could control so many clubs, he was sure he could afford better paint to huff.

People had formed a circle around him. At first, he thought he'd done something gross and wrong again, but everyone was paying attention to him, clapping and cheering him on.

He realized he was humping the air and he had that wonderful feeling in his crotch again.

The music and the heat from the people around him drove him into a frenzy and he thrust against the air until he ejaculated another meat wad from his penis. It slapped onto the floor and went scuttling off into the crowd. An obese woman shrieked and punched her way to the center of the floor.

"It's eating her meat photo!" someone shouted.

"Do something!" someone else shouted.

Tony pulled his lighter out of his ass and said, "Anybody got any spray paint?"

Someone handed him a can of spray paint. He aimed it at the meat he'd ejaculated, sparked the lighter, and blew a jet of flame at the woman's face. The hunk of meat charred and dropped from the woman's face, revealing the tattered remains of her meat photo.

Tony felt like he'd done something good, but immediately dropped to his knees and began humping the air.

He heard someone nearby say, "That thing came from him. He's going to do it again."

Somebody else said, "He's coming meat and that meat wants our meat photos."

Tony tried to listen to them, tried to make sense of it, but he couldn't focus on anything but that sensation building in his stiff penis.

"He doesn't belong here," someone else said.

Tony raised his head to the rafters and screamed as he ejaculated another wad of meat.

"Get it before it gets somebody else," a man with an excessive amount of pubic hair said.

A number of people went charging after the meat wad. But soon everyone was distracted by something else.

Tony, on his knees, followed everyone's gaze as a large man cut his way through the crowd.

Right away, Tony realized this man was covered in the one true meat photo. It covered his torso and commanded everyone in the room's attention. Or the attention could've been from the man's exposed penis protruding from the photo. Either way, all eyes were on the newcomer. A smaller replication of the large, framed photo covered the man's face.

The man opened his arms wide and said, "I am Ancient Evil. I will be your salvation."

Tony, who didn't know the meaning of a lot of words, was still confused by what the man said. Like, was he evil or was that just his name? Dumb name if it was.

But Tony couldn't concern himself with that. He needed to hide. His meat photo mask was commanding him to do it. He needed to find someplace away from this interloper and ejaculate as many hunks of meat as he possibly could. He looked down at his penis. The tip was red, swollen, and emitted a yellowish discharge.

Ancient Evil pointed at him. "He is the dispenser of false meat!"

Tony got to his feet and ran, in search of the darkest corner he could find.

# 46

NEAL LITTLE SAT IN THE back room of the Dollar General reading *Retail World Magazine*. All his beautiful photos of meat were gone. It was his life's work and now that he couldn't look at it every day he felt empty and hollow. He'd tried to replace the feeling of accomplishment by painting the Dollar General but it wasn't the same. Besides, it wasn't his anymore.

He'd let Tony start Club Meat even though Neal hated dancing. It was a jealousy thing. Neal had tried to learn how to dance when he was twelve but his friends had made fun of him. He went to a school dance and ended up being a wallflower. He'd watched all the other kids sway to the slow music and had thought it didn't look that hard and eventually got up the nerve to ask a cute girl from his class to dance with him. Neal ended up stomping all over the girl's feet while a group of his friends laughed at him. He ended up crying and running all the way home.

As the years went by, Neal resented people when he saw them dancing. They all looked so happy or were really good. He never went to weddings or clubs or anywhere he thought people might spontaneously break into dance.

Neal decided to keep himself busy in back of the store and away from all the people who were having a good time and dancing. He'd dug around in the junk left behind and had found a stack of *Retail World Magazine*. The articles were pretty interesting. There were tips on how to start your own franchise, how to boost employee morale, how to chart your inventory, and how to market your store. He began to think that maybe returning the Dollar General back into a store might be a more lucrative prospect. He really needed to contemplate doing something new with his life.

Tony hadn't charged anyone to enter the club. And none of the people who'd come had appreciated his mural. Maybe it was time to switch professions and start a lucrative career in retail.

Neal was so ensconced in the thought of becoming a manager— or possibly the owner—of a Dollar General that he didn't notice when all the screaming began.

# 47

**T**ONY COWERED IN A CORNER at the back of the store. He couldn't control his hips as they pumped the air and his penis began to swell again.

"He's doing it again!" someone yelled.

"He's a false prophet!" Ancient Evil bellowed. "You must kill him and bring me his meat photo! Only I can save you!"

The crowd began to swarm Tony. He screamed as several wads of meat exploded from his penis and slapped the faces of several people closing in on him. Before he could recover, another explosion of meat hit the crowd.

"I can't stop humping!" Tony tried to scream over the panicked crowd.

Another ejaculation of meat shredded Tony's penis and left a gaping hole where it had once been. Meat began to spill out of the hole. People screamed and tried to get away as the meat that fell to the floor shot through the air and began to attack everyone's meat photos.

Ancient Evil screamed out of frustration and began to absorb the people closest to him, trying to clear a path to Tony. After he'd absorbed some of the crowd, he felt something sharp shoot from his anus. He stopped and felt his anus. It felt wet. He looked at his fingers. There was blood on them. He tried to look at his own ass, which was impossible, but spotted something on the floor behind him. On the floor was a fresh meat photo with a smear of blood on the border. He knew the photo had given him a papercut on his anus. This infuriated Ancient Evil even more.

He turned back toward the crowd and began to absorb more people. They were practically running toward him now, trying to get away from Tony and his false meat. He didn't even need to chase them. As each person was absorbed, several meat photos shot from his ass, adding more papercuts to his sphincter as they entered the world. He knew he had to get Tony's photo. He had to stop this madness and be the one and true owner of all the meat photos.

Ancient Evil grew and the power of his meat photo began to open the portal within him further. His meat photo began to swirl.

An attractive young woman near him held a hunk of meat and was punching it, trying to keep it from attaching to her meat photo. She suddenly looked to the door of Club Meat and said, "I can't believe it. It can't be," before she lost her battle with the slab of meat and it attached to her face. The meat made slurping sounds as it worked.

"Oh my god! I can't believe it!" a man said. "It's Nicolas Cage! Man, I hate that guy's face so much! He makes that same dumb, slack-jaw expression in every movie he's in!"

Ancient Evil spun toward the door, shooting a confetti of meat photos over the crowd as he did so. His ass felt like it was on fire. Sure enough, Nicolas Cage stood at the door of the Dollar General, scanning the scene with that dumb, open-mouthed, confused expression he always wore. And beside him stood the handsome Keanu Reeves. Ancient Evil roared as his meat photo pulled both of them in. He hated Nicolas Cage's face even more the closer he got. He felt good ridding the world of that dumb fucking face.

After absorbing both of the celebrities, a steady stream of meat photos spilled from Ancient Evil's ass. He couldn't stop them from coming if he tried. The papercuts were excruciating but he was growing numb to the pain. It was all for the greater good that his anus was being obliterated. It was all part of world domination. It was part of the Great Migration. There was no pain when you were a god.

Ancient Evil opened his arms and pulled as hard as he could. Everyone in the room was lifted from their feet and pulled into his meat photo. Everyone except for Tony.

Tony was still crouched in a corner and humping the air, piles of meat spilling on the floor and scrambling toward the photos steadily shooting from Ancient Evil's ass.

"You!" Ancient Evil said. "Your mask is false! I'm the one true meat photo! I am the savior!"

Ancient Evil opened his arms. The meat on his photo swirled and flashes of light resembling lightning raced over the glistening meat. He strained and his veins rose to the surface of his skin. His skin was so tight from his bulk that it threatened to split. The meat photos were shooting from his anus like a money counter, piling up on the floor behind him. The red light in the room grew brighter.

Tony screamed as the meat photo attached to his face began to stretch as it was pulled toward Ancient Evil. Tony still couldn't stop humping but his meat ejaculate was starting to slow. The skin on Tony's face stretched as he dug his fingers into the concrete wall behind him.

A ripping sound tore through the now empty Dollar General and Tony watched as not only the meat covering his face but all the flesh from his skull was sucked into Ancient Evil. He screamed as the pain raced through his face but stopped when the nerves were severed.

Ancient Evil stood triumphant in the middle of the Dollar General. It hadn't been that long ago he'd become aware of his mission and now he felt that mission was accomplished.

He looked at the boy whose head was only a skull and said, "You're safe now. The false photo is gone from this world."

Tony looked around the club, thinking there must be a cigarette somewhere. He couldn't remember where he'd put his pack.

He wasn't watching when Ancient Evil, having absorbed everyone in the club and the false meat—the *real* ancient evil—pulled his penis from the large meat photo and removed it from his torso, placed it flat on the floor, and disappeared into it.

Ancient Evil had thought about saying, "I'll return when needed," but no one seemed to be listening so he didn't bother.

# 48

*RETAIL WORLD MAGAZINE* **HAD GOTTEN** so boring Neal didn't think he could read any more. He was pretty sure the five pages or so he'd read had given him enough of a blueprint to start another Dollar General. He felt like he'd probably have to get some sort of franchising license to do that and that sounded like a lot of work. He thought maybe he could call it Two-Dollar General and that his future customers would feel superior to Dollar General customers, but he didn't want to be accused of catering to the elite.

He listened for the sounds of the club from the back of the store, but it sounded like things had quieted down. If Tony were still out there, maybe he could ask what he thought of the idea. After all, if Neal was going to open a slightly less discount store, he wanted to be around for a while and someone as young as Tony could provide him with valuable knowledge about that demographic.

He noticed Tony's pack of cigarettes on the corner of his desk. He was surprised the boy hadn't come back for them. As the boy's default caregiver, this worried Neal.

He picked up the pack of cigarettes—only one left—and walked back out into the store, expecting to see at least the aftermath of a party.

What he saw was something else.

The place was littered with meat photos and in the middle of all of them was a larger one that glistened and shone more than the rest. He stared at the large, framed photo and noticed a tear in it. The hole slowly sealed itself shut and Neal knew that it was something special.

Neal no longer wanted to be a retail store mogul. His true purpose in life had been renewed. He would start the museum again. He would be the keeper of the meat photos. He'd take donations but wouldn't sell a single one.

Shaking with excitement, he bent to pick up the oversized meat photo. He could feel the power radiating from it.

"Yeah, that's a nice one," Tony said from behind. He sounded different.

Neal turned to him and leapt back when he saw that the kid had absolutely no flesh on his skull.

"Got a cigarette?" the boy said.

Neal held out the mostly empty pack of cigarettes and a lighter to the boy.

He watched as Tony tried to put the cigarette in his mouth but, with no lips, he had to clamp down on it with his teeth.

Neal lit the cigarette for him but, with no cheeks, Tony couldn't get a good draw on it. He let the cigarette tumble out of his mouth and smashed it out with his bare foot.

"Even smoking sucks now," Tony said. "I'm not even gonna be able to huff."

Neal, his mind a million miles away, said, "Maybe it's time to get into pills."

"I'm gonna go out and watch the sun come up. Think about things."

Neal followed the boy to the front door. After Tony exited the building, Neal locked the doors so he could be alone in the Dollar General. It didn't matter that all the glass in the door had been shattered. It was the symbolism that counted.

He turned back to the work at hand, that stack of meat photos.

They were all his.

For the first time in his life, he felt powerful. He looked around the store and said, "Meat photo."

**Other Grindhouse Press Titles**

#666__*Satanic Summer* by Andersen Prunty

#086__*Dreaditation* by Andersen Prunty

#085__*The Unseen II* by Bryan Smith

#084__*Waif* by Samantha Kolesnik

#083__*Racing with the Devil* by Bryan Smith

#082__*Bodies Wrapped in Plastic and Other Items of Interest* by Andersen Prunty

#081__*The Next Time You See Me I'll Probably Be Dead* by C.V. Hunt

#080__*The Unseen* by Bryan Smith

#079__*The Late Night Horror Show* by Bryan Smith

#078__*Birth of a Monster* by A.S. Coomer

#077__*Invitation to Death* by Bryan Smith

#076__*Paradise Club* by Tim Meyer

#075__*Mage of the Hellmouth* by John Wayne Comunale

#074__*The Rotting Within* by Matt Kurtz

#073__*Go Down Hard* by Ali Seay

#072__*Girl of Prey* by Pete Risley

#071__*Gone to See the River Man* by Kristopher Triana

#070__*Horrorama* edited by C.V. Hunt

#069__*Depraved 4* by Bryan Smith

#068__*Worst Laid Plans: An Anthology of Vacation Horror* edited by Samantha Kolesnik

#067__*Deathtripping: Collected Horror Stories* by Andersen Prunty

#066__*Depraved* by Bryan Smith

#065__*Crazytimes* by Scott Cole

#064__*Blood Relations* by Kristopher Triana

#063__*The Perfectly Fine House* by Stephen Kozeniewski and Wile E. Young

#062__*Savage Mountain* by John Quick

#061__*Cocksucker* by Lucas Milliron

#060__*Luciferin* by J. Peter W.

#059__*The Fucking Zombie Apocalypse* by Bryan Smith

#058__*True Crime* by Samantha Kolesnik

#057__*The Cycle* by John Wayne Comunale

#056__*A Voice So Soft* by Patrick Lacey

#055__*Merciless* by Bryan Smith

#054__*The Long Shadows of October* by Kristopher Triana

#053__*House of Blood* by Bryan Smith

#052__*The Freakshow* by Bryan Smith

#051__*Dirty Rotten Hippies and Other Stories* by Bryan Smith

#050__*Rites of Extinction* by Matt Serafini

#049__*Saint Sadist* by Lucas Mangum

#048__*Neon Dies at Dawn* by Andersen Prunty

#047__*Halloween Fiend* by C.V. Hunt

#046__*Limbs: A Love Story* by Tim Meyer

#045__*As Seen On T.V.* by John Wayne Comunale

#044__*Where Stars Won't Shine* by Patrick Lacey

#043__*Kinfolk* by Matt Kurtz

#042__*Kill For Satan!* by Bryan Smith

#041__*Dead Stripper Storage* by Bryan Smith

#040__*Triple Axe* by Scott Cole

#039__*Scummer* by John Wayne Comunale

#038__*Cockblock* by C.V. Hunt

#037__*Irrationalia* by Andersen Prunty

#036__*Full Brutal* by Kristopher Triana

#035__*Office Mutant* by Pete Risley

#034__*Death Pacts and Left-Hand Paths* by John Wayne Comunale

#033__*Home Is Where the Horror Is* by C.V. Hunt

#032__*This Town Needs A Monster* by Andersen Prunty

#031__*The Fetishists* by A.S. Coomer

#030__*Ritualistic Human Sacrifice* by C.V. Hunt

#029__*The Atrocity Vendor* by Nick Cato

#028__*Burn Down the House and Everyone In It* by Zachary T. Owen

#027__*Misery and Death and Everything Depressing* by C.V. Hunt

#026__*Naked Friends* by Justin Grimbol

#025__*Ghost Chant* by Gina Ranalli

#024__*Hearers of the Constant Hum* by William Pauley III

#023__*Hell's Waiting Room* by C.V. Hunt

#022__*Creep House: Horror Stories* by Andersen Prunty

#021__*Other People's Shit* by C.V. Hunt

#020__*The Party Lords* by Justin Grimbol

#019__*Sociopaths In Love* by Andersen Prunty

#018__*The Last Porno Theater* by Nick Cato

#017__*Zombieville* by C.V. Hunt

#016__*Samurai Vs. Robo-Dick* by Steve Lowe

#015__*The Warm Glow of Happy Homes* by Andersen Prunty

#014__*How To Kill Yourself* by C.V. Hunt

#013__*Bury the Children in the Yard: Horror Stories* by Andersen Prunty

#012__*Return to Devil Town (Vampires in Devil Town Book Three)* by Wayne Hixon

#011__*Pray You Die Alone: Horror Stories* by Andersen Prunty

#010__*King of the Perverts* by Steve Lowe

#009__*Sunruined: Horror Stories* by Andersen Prunty

#008__*Bright Black Moon (Vampires in Devil Town Book Two)* by Wayne Hixon

#007__*Hi I'm a Social Disease: Horror Stories* by Andersen Prunty

#006__*A Life On Fire* by Chris Bowsman

#005__*The Sorrow King* by Andersen Prunty

#004__*The Brothers Crunk* by William Pauley III

#003__*The Horribles* by Nathaniel Lambert

#002__*Vampires in Devil Town* by Wayne Hixon

#001__*House of Fallen Trees* by Gina Ranalli

#000__*Morning is Dead* by Andersen Prunty

www.ingramcontent.com/pod-product-compliance
Lightning Source LLC
Chambersburg PA
CBHW011436240626
47153CB00011B/3019